SPECIMEN

MICHAEL COLE

RAVEN TALE
PUBLISHING

1

They were down to three men.

When Lijun was recruited into the secret Red Lightning, he saw it as an honor. A dedicated special ops force, designed to protect national interests against the regressive and corrupt western world, it hired only the best men. Off the books, they infiltrated nations and agencies around the globe. It was said to be an integral part of the homeland's quest for global superiority. Sabotage, intel, weapons research—the Red Lightning did it all. And when it came time to strike, their enemies never knew what hit them.

Never did Lijun know that *he* would be the next casualty in this crusade.

All he was supposed to do was security: monitor the shorelines, watch the skies, keep the scientists in line. For a man of his expertise, it was as simple an assignment as they came. All he knew about the project was that it was centered around weapons research. Bioweapons, to be precise. What kind of bioweapons? Lijun didn't ask. As long as it was effective against his country's enemies, he didn't care.

At noon, he heard the alarm go off.

CONTAINMENT BREACH!

What followed was a marathon of chaos and confusion. The staff, acting against orders—against *protocol*—were evacuating the lab. As soon as Lijun arrived, he heard gunfire and screams. When he entered the lab, he found a hole in the ceiling and blood on the floor.

The scientists were successful. *Too* successful. They had created something so deadly, it couldn't be contained or controlled.

Now, it was outside. Lijun, a man who was used to being the hunter, was now the prey.

Five minutes ago, he had lost contact with the station's commander. The gunfire to the southwest had gone eerily silent, as had the screams. These were strikers, the fighting arm of the Red Lightning. They were not ones to go down easily.

The trio of strikers looked to the south, then at each other. Fabin was the oldest of the three. A trained paratrooper, he was not easily fazed by dangerous circumstances. Today, however, he was visibly unnerved. He tried not to show it, but the truth was plain in his eyes.

The same was true for Haoxuan. He was younger than the others and much more bull-headed. He was not sensitive to death. In fact, he took a sick pleasure in it. It was part of the training process. This was not a profession that nurtured a good conscience. These strikers were born to serve the Red Lightning by any means necessary, including sabotage and murder.

Now, it was their own forces who were getting massacred. Each man knew he would soon be next.

"It's quiet," Haoxuan said.

"That's what bothers me," Fabin replied.

"You think the commander is alive?" Haoxuan asked.

Lijun shook his head. "Not likely."

Fabin glanced at the surrounding jungle. "Running's no good. We need a plan. Or else, we may as well roll over and die."

"I hate to say it, sir, but that might be the better option." Lijun braced for the inevitable backlash. Despite the sergeant's obvious fear, his sense of loyalty remained. He struck Lijun with a glare and snarl . . . then with a blow to the chin.

Next thing Lijun knew, he was on the ground with Fabin standing over him. His submachine gun was pointed at Lijun's head, ready to punish him for his cowardice. After all his training, after taking the pay, accepting the gifts—including young women ordered by the regime to serve its strikers—Lijun was unwilling to perform his duty to the max.

As far as Lijun was concerned, it had nothing to do with a lack of loyalty and everything to do with basic facts. Dying for his country was one thing. Suffering a slow, painful, gruesome death was another. They had seen the larvae. They saw what they did to their prey. Lijun wanted no part of that. In fact, he would rather take the bullet.

"I should shoot you right now," Fabin said.

Lijun remained silent, his eyes fixed on the muzzle of that submachine gun. For the first time, he felt the shadow of death casting over him. At first, he was fearful. A few moments later, he was at peace. All he had to do was accept the facts. Rescue was unlikely to come. The government would probably abandon this project after learning of this outbreak.

Death was coming whether Lijun wanted it to or not. At least he had a choice of how he would go out. A bullet sounded much better than being slowly devoured.

"Go ahead," he said. He tilted his head at the jungle behind him. "You hear that? . . . Oh, you don't? That's right. Our security forces have already faltered. The freaks in the lab have done their job a little too well. The weapon works, and it has no loyalty to the homeland. Our men are dead, and we're next. I think we only have one option."

"Oh, the coward is making suggestions." Fabin said. "And what exactly does the coward recommend we do?"

Lijun looked the sergeant in the eye, then over at Haoxuan. The young striker was clenching his teeth in fear. Not of the experiment, but the wrath of his sergeant. Already, Lijun knew whatever he said would fall on deaf ears. Still, he figured he may as well say his piece.

"We know what fate awaits us. I say we put our guns to our own heads and pull the trigger. You call it cowardice. I call it smart."

Fabin spat on him. "Cowardice it is. After all the Red Lightning has given you, you show your true colors. No, you will not die by the bullet. At least, not your own. You will die retaking the lab and recapturing the experiment. If you don't, I will kill you myself."

A kick to the side reinforced the point.

Lijun stayed in place, now clutching his ribs. It was a simple thought process. Either he shot himself, or Fabin shot him. Either method was better than the alternative.

Fabin kicked him again. "Get up, coward!"

Lijun shook his head.

Fabin took aim. "Now."

"On your feet," Haoxuan said.

Lijun gave the young striker a pitiful glance. The propaganda heavily influenced the young. Lijun reflected on his twenty-year-old self. His last act of free will was joining the military. Since then, he had been a machine, mindlessly obeying the will of people who would send him to his death without a moment's consideration. Only now, with death lurking around the corner, did Lijun find something he did not even realize he'd been craving his entire adult life—his free will.

"Do it," he said. "What are you waiting for, Fabin? Shoot me! What's taking so long? You going to soil yourself? Pull the trigger, you damn coward."

His choice of words had the desired effect. Fabin, sneering like an angry canine, looked down the iron sights of his gun and began applying pressure to the trigger.

Gunshots rang in their ears.

Lijun and Fabin turned just in time to see the screaming Haoxuan being lifted into the trees. His submachine gun hit the ground, its mag half-full. The leaves shook, the screaming continuing for another few moments before peaking with an agonized squeal. Silence followed.

Only for a moment.

Fabin shifted his aim, ready to unload into the canopy. "Come on, you filthy bug. Come get me!"

He didn't expect to have his challenge answered so quickly. In a blur of motion, the creature's black body descended from the tree BEHIND Fabin.

His head shot back, his arms extending outward as he arched back. The long, segmented tail pushed its spear-tip out of his stomach. Skewered, the sergeant looked at the pointed tip, which was dripping venom. The creature was a little too eager to kill: it often struck too hard with its stinger.

With blood dripping from his mouth and torso, Fabin received the very thing Lijun wanted: a relatively quick death.

Lijun picked up his submachine gun. For a split second, he debated whether to shoot himself or the creature. It was right there in plain sight. It was an easy shot, one that could make him revered as a hero by any other surviving strikers. It would even get him recognized by high-ranking military officers in charge of the project. He might even see a promotion that would put him in charge of the next project.

His indecisiveness proved to be his downfall. The creature

tossed Fabin's warm corpse aside, closed the distance, and struck.

This time, it stung with appropriate force. The stinger entered Lijun's abdomen, immediately pumping him full of paralyzing toxins.

Lijun lay there in pain and shock. He tried to squeeze the trigger, but nothing was happening. It was as though his body refused to function. He was on the ground, unable to move, speak, or even swallow. His heart beat slowly, his lungs continuing to function. It was an automatic process, the same as if he was asleep.

All he could control was his mind, which was quickly spiraling out of control. Madness and self-loathing consumed his thoughts.

That precious free will he had discovered had sealed his fate. Had he remained the disciplined striker, he may have shot the creature immediately.

He felt his body scrape against the earth as the creature dragged him to its nest. To his slow, agonizing fate.

Lijun tried to scream but couldn't. All he wanted was to trade places with the deceased Fabin. The sergeant would never know how lucky he was.

Lijun, on the other hand, would know all too well.

2

To the rest of the world, he was a ghost. Most of those who saw his face had their eyes shut permanently. War was his life. Training and forging weapons were his pastime. To him, deployment was as natural as punching a timesheet.

His parents had given him an honorable name at birth. Nobody, not even his squad, and especially not his clients, knew what it was. To them, he was simply known as Whitmore.

At age eighteen, he joined the U.S. Army. At nineteen, he entered Ranger School. That same year, he took part in his first combat mission. It was then when Whitmore bagged his first confirmed kills. Two insurgents were dead by his hand, saving the lives of two of his fellow soldiers. The rescue mission was successful, earning Whitmore a promotion and more dangerous assignments. After twenty years, not only was Whitmore even more battle-hardened, but he had grown to be business savvy.

During his deployments, he had the privilege of working with government contractors. Some were on the books; others were not. Both were paid substantially more than even a sergeant major in the U.S. Army. Better yet, those off the books did not operate by the same bullshit rules of engagement. There was no red tape or permission-asking. Just an objective and a result.

With this in mind, Whitmore officially retired. Then, the real money-making began.

The jobs took him to places where he never thought he'd see combat, and to places that were all too familiar. Every operation was a success, leading to more job offers. His clientele ranged from private individuals to the U.S. government. The latter tended to pay the best.

Forty-eight hours ago, they had contacted him, immediately getting his attention with their generous pay offer.

The job was straightforward: escort a CIA agent to an island in the South China Sea, kill all enemy combatants, and retrieve any available computer data and lab samples. Whitmore was uncertain what the latter was exactly, but then again, that was the point. The CIA did not want him to know what it was, and more importantly, they did not want any other countries to have it—whatever *it* was. That alone told Whitmore all he needed to know.

His mind was focused on the meat of this operation—that being the meat he would grind to get the job done. In this instance, that meat was known as the Red Lightning.

The United States was not the only nation that used *unofficial* contractors to achieve its devious goals. It did not matter that the Red Lightning's employer just so happened to own the means of production and every industry within its borders. On paper, it was a separate entity altogether. Whitmore understood the deal. If the so-called contractor was caught, the government could deny any involvement. It was no different than Whitmore's seemingly daily life.

The only difference was he never got caught.

· · ·

As far as the rest of the world was concerned, the *USS Schaefer* was on a routine patrol in the South China Sea. On paper, the SH-60 Sea Hawk was delivering supplies to a cruiser forty miles northeast of its current location.

Twenty miles into the flight, Whitmore and his team made their deployment. What followed was a three-mile swim to an island called South Fire. On a map, the island resembled an upside-down torch. Its upper region, which was slanted northeast, was rod-shaped, the shoreline relatively smooth. The southwest end, however, was lined with razor-sharp rocks and oddly shaped, pointed peninsulas. On a satellite image, it resembled an illustration of grayish-green flame.

Whitmore didn't mind the swim. He had been in colder waters than this on plenty of occasions. In addition, he thought of it as a nice warm-up exercise preceding the meat grinding.

As he entered the shallows, he abandoned his diver propulsion vehicle and went ashore. Crossing several yards of rigid seabed, he kept his eyes on the island. So far, there were no sentries or lookouts. That was somewhat surprising. If he was in charge of security for a secret operation such as this, he would have had lookouts every few yards. Maybe the Red Lightning was not what they were cracked up to be.

Whitmore set foot ashore and unpacked his main weapon of choice, an M16A2 with an under-barrel grenade launcher. For the next few seconds, he kept watch while the rest of his team arrived.

The first was Jie Lee, the CIA liaison. Thirty-five years old, he managed to keep up with the mercenaries. Whitmore was never thrilled about escorting agents. Either they failed to keep up, or they tried to take charge of the mission. According to the briefing, Lee had served as a U.S. Marine for four years before getting recruited by the agency. For three years, he had worked undercover in an undisclosed region in Asia. The secrecy nearly made Whitmore and his team laugh. As if the country wasn't obvious. Regardless, Lee had infiltrated the Red Lightning and found evidence of their activities, including bioweapons research. As it turned out, they had been responsible for numerous cyberattacks in the U.S. and U.K., as well as responsible for the sinking of an American research vessel in the South Pacific. Whatever it was that the team was researching, Whitmore did not know. But it was clear the Red Lightning was not happy about it.

Next to emerge was Brook, an expert sniper with over forty confirmed kills from his many active-duty deployments. But it wasn't his sniper skills that Whitmore found most useful, but rather his tracking skills. From both his early hunting days in the woodlands of Montana and his eight years in the Army, Brook was trained to recognize any and every imprint in the earth. Whether he was tracking a human or an animal, he could describe its entire journey based on the signs it left behind.

Of course, his skill with weaponry also proved useful. Today, instead of a sniper rifle, the dark-haired former rancher went with an M4A1 Carbine.

Two more men emerged. Sporting a broken-toothed snarl was Trent. Not many had had the pleasure of escaping a Taliban prison camp, while also killing all the enemy soldiers guarding it. After reaching an American base, the Marine went straight back into combat duty, armed with some fresh intel on an enemy stronghold.

Delta, sporting a green boonie hat, arrived beside him. The team's explosives expert, he was looking forward to turning the alleged bio-lab into a fireworks show. In a team of quiet, reserved men, he was the one with a set of jaws that never seemed to stay shut. None of his jokes were good. Most were cringy and annoying, as a matter of fact. Luckily, Whitmore had not hired him for his skill as a comedian.

As the men prepped themselves to infiltrate the island, the last two teammates arrived. The first was Zed, his thick mustache covering his entire upper lip. For many evil men across the globe, that mustache was the last thing they ever saw.

Then there was Gerry. With skin as dark as death, he functioned best on moonless nights and in thick canopy. Often, his victims *never* saw him. It was a genetic gift, and a curse to his enemies.

The team of seven geared up, hid their supplies, then disappeared into the jungle.

As usual, Delta was the first to open his mouth.

"No welcome party?"

The men followed Whitmore's hand signals and fanned out, forming a perimeter. They checked for flares, claymores, and surveillance equipment.

Zed made a bird-like whistle, alerting his teammates to a camera positioned on a tree branch. Brook silently approached the tree. He climbed the opposite side of its trunk, then reached around to get at the device. Finding its wireless transmitter and receiver, he planted a tiny signal disruptor.

Lee approached with a tablet in hand. Of course, this wasn't some electronic device someone bought from Best Buy. No, this was spy shit. He hacked into the camera's signal, which allowed the device to detect other wireless signals of the same frequency, in turn allowing him to detect other security cameras across the island.

"They're mainly placed along the jungle perimeter," he said to Whitmore.

"You can disable them with that thing?" Whitmore asked.

"If I can get close enough, yes," Lee said.

Whitmore looked to Gerry and Zed. Both men had identified some trip flares and disabled them.

It was odd to see this much effort in securing the island

perimeter, yet there wasn't a single sentry on patrol. Regardless, it was clear the people on this island absolutely did not want visitors.

"Flight area and docks are about half a klick northeast," Lee said. "Just beyond the torch."

Whitmore looked at Brook, then tilted his head northeast.

Brook took point, quickly disappearing into the distance. The rest of the team followed. The lack of hostiles meant nothing. As far as they knew, this island was hell's idea of paradise.

They made their way to the dock area. The first part of the mission: disable the radio tower and all vehicles. And, of course, eliminate any strikers they found.

3

The thing Whitmore hated most when in enemy territory was silence. So far, they had yet to come across a striker patrol, even as they neared the dock area. No way were these guys *that* incompetent. Only a few explanations made sense. Perhaps the Red Lightning was aware of the team's presence and was preparing an ambush.

The environment supported that theory. The island's flora, consisting of Siamese sal trees, sapwood trees, and some green undergrowth between them, all allowed for good cover while also being spacious enough to allow for decent visibility.

A second theory was that perhaps something had gone seriously wrong on this island. Maybe the security personnel were gathered elsewhere. For now, all Whitmore knew for sure was that something did not feel right.

That feeling was perpetuated by the sight of birds flying offshore, escaping into the horizon. AWAY from the island. At least three times since coming ashore had Whitmore noticed this. He knew what feeding behavior in tropical birds looked like. This wasn't it.

As the team closed within seven hundred meters of the docks, it became apparent that the second theory was correct.

It started with the discovery of a few dead bugs. Beetles, some as large as six inches in length. With a land mass of over twelve square miles, South Fire was home to more wildlife than many other islands in the South China Sea. Birds, lizards, insects, occasionally some walruses, and even primates lived here.

A couple dead bugs wasn't considered odd. Hundreds of them, on the other hand, was more bizarre. It wasn't just beetles. Dead birds were scattered everywhere. Scorpions, spiders, snakes, worms, moths: all lay in the ferns and dirt in various stages of decay.

The shrubs and ferns were wilted and discolored. Their natural green, yellow, and red pigments had turned into shades of brown. Scattered across this graveyard of flora and fauna were multiple canisters of poison.

Whitmore halted his team and began to inspect the findings. Zed picked up one of the canisters.

"Pesticide." He tossed the canister to Whitmore. The mercenary leader gave the can a glance, then handed it to Lee.

"Mean anything to you?"

Lee looked at the label on the metal canister, then at the vast display of death. At least a dozen of these cans were in plain sight, laying all over the surrounding jungle.

"It's a pesticide. They killed a lot of pests," he said.

Whitmore kept his eyes on the agent. This was another reason he hated babysitting government spooks. They always gave bullshit answers.

"This much poison? This far from the barracks and the lab?" he said. "Looks like they specifically targeted this area. Either they really like killing wildlife, or they were commencing a targeted attack using chemicals."

"Sir!"

Whitmore turned to Gerry, who was waving him over to the northwest corner of this valley of death. He approached, finding Gerry looking at larger casualties of the Red Lightning's actions.

Laying on the ground were three large boars. Two of them were males, sporting four-inch tusks and weighing two hundred pounds. The third was a female, weighing around one-seventy.

It was a strange sight. These creatures were not killed by the poison gas, but rather multiple shots to the head and center mass. Massive craters in their flesh revealed the inside of their skulls and torsos. For creatures of this size, only one or two bullets would have been necessary to inflict death. This was not hunting, nor did it appear to be self-defense. The strikers had deliberately shot these animals repeatedly.

And there was no doubt it was strikers who did this. Littering the earth were the shell casings from 5.45x39mm bullets. The Red Lightning's primary infantry weapon was believed to be the AK-74, purchased from the Russian military.

Gerry glanced at the sergeant major and shook his head. "Maybe the sick fucks were bored."

Whitmore nodded. "Maybe." He looked at the dead bugs and birds, then turned his gaze back to the boars. "Or they're purposely exterminating all animal life on the island. It's a common response whenever there's an outbreak. Chernobyl, for example."

"That lab in Syria . . ." Gerry muttered.

Whitmore nodded. It was an unfortunate aspect of the job, covering up secrets. Bioresearch was all the rage these days, it seemed. As much as governments loved their nuclear weapons, they carried too large a risk for conventional use. One launch could lead to a thousand. Nobody wins. Even those with bunkers would have to face the famine. Bioweapons, however, if deployed right, could result in mass death without being traced back to the aggressor. They could even be mistaken for a naturally occurring phenomenon.

On more than one occasion, Whitmore's team had been recruited to erase evidence of a certain government's involvement in such facilities. Whitmore never lost sleep over it. Not anymore. It was the way of the world.

Brook approached from the northeast. "Sergeant Major."

"What did you find?" Whitmore asked.

Brook tilted his head toward the boars. "It was five men. They ran in from the northwest. Deployed the canisters, after killing the boars. They were in a hurry." He pointed his elbow at the ground a few yards behind them. "They engaged in another brief firefight, then took off toward the docks."

Whitmore looked at Lee. "You know of any other teams being sent in?"

"Negative," Lee said.

Whitmore kept an inquisitive stare on him. When they'd first met, Lee demonstrated a suave demeanor. He was confident. Cocky, even. The guy had spent multiple years undercover as a spy, gathering intel on groups who would have killed him slowly and painfully had his cover been blown.

Now, he was a far cry from that guy in the conference room back at Langley. He was sweating, his jaw slightly agape. Whitmore knew the look of fear when he saw it.

"There's something else," Brook said. He led Whitmore and Lee to the center of the firefight. Bullet casings littered the ground, but there was no sign of return fire. The only damage to the smaller plant life was either chemical or crushing by army boots.

Brook pointed to the tree. Its trunk had been splintered by multiple bullet hits. One of the branches hung by a few splinters of wood, having taken the brunt of the impacts.

Whitmore didn't need Brook to explain. Those men had been shooting into the tree.

None of it added up. First, the strikers gassed the hell out of the area, then brutally gunned down some wild boar, and then engaged in a firefight with an enemy perched within the tree, before retreating to the docks.

Combine all that with the fact they hadn't found a single striker so far, and everything screamed 'outbreak.'

"Sir, if I may?" Delta said.

"Go ahead," Whitmore said.

Delta looked at Lee. "The shit they were experimenting with . . . it's not something we're gonna catch by breathing in, is it?"

"No," Lee said. "It's not chemical in nature."

"Well, regardless, I'm starting to think we're in our right to know what it is," Whitmore said.

As he expected, the agent shook his head.

"Let's continue on," Lee said. "For all we know, it's been contained. Let's hit the docks, then move on to the lab. Faster we do this—"

"You can fuck off with the motivational talk," Delta said. That shut Lee up.

Whitmore knew he wasn't going to get any answers. All he could do for now was focus on the certainties. One of which was the trail that led to the dock area. More than likely, they would finally encounter some enemy hostiles there.

"Move out. Stay silent."

Silent as ghosts, the team continued north.

4

"Balance."

He planted his feet on the ground. His eyes were on the river. Just a few inches underneath was a fifteen-inch carp.

"Form your T-stance."

He shifted his left leg toward the bug, using his throwing arm to keep himself steady.

"Breathe. Breathe." His father's voice was calm and slow. "Do not take your eyes off of the fish. Balance and breathe. Let everything disappear except you and your target. Focus ..."

He inhaled through his nose, his eyes fixed on the carp. It was smaller than the ones his father used to spear on the northern bend of the river. He worried he would not be able to put the tip of the spear through it. He had missed larger targets before.

"Breathe. It doesn't know you're here. Twist your hips. Let your arm follow through. Your body will do the work."

He took a deep breath and let the rest of the world fade out. It was only him and the fish.

The time was now.

He threw the spear. The fish did not know what hit it. The barb had struck behind the gill slit.

"Well done."

The memory recurred every now and then. A fragment of what Whitmore considered to be his first life, it infiltrated his mind like a virus. Spearfishing on the lake was his dad's favorite pastime, a skill learned during his own youth. It was a time of innocence and youth. A different time, in which he was a much different man.

So different, that he refused to reflect on those memories, for that version of him was incompatible with the man he had become. He saw himself as a man of war, always chasing the next fight. So much so, that he had forgotten the notion of peace.

He forced the memory into a chasm where all forgotten things were discarded. That young man did not exist anymore. Only Whitmore remained. All that mattered was his second life. His *current* life. That, and the mission at hand.

In the span of a heartbeat, he was back in reality.

As THE TEAM came within one hundred meters of the docks, they were hit with the smell of burnt diesel fuel and metal. At fifty meters, the smell of burnt flesh and gunpowder joined the hodgepodge of aromas. Already, it was clear—the findings in the jungle were only a hint of the disaster that had swept the island.

Four patrol boats, armed with fifty-caliber machine guns, were docked at the shoreline. Two others were sunk several meters offshore, their bows pointing skyward above the shallow water. Even from this distance, the damage to their hulls was plain as day. Both vessels had been bombarded with rifle fire and RPGs. They were undoubtedly the same model as the other boats, meaning they were owned by the Red Lightning. It did not appear to have been the result of an incoming attack, but rather an attempt to prevent the boats from leaving.

The observation of the rest of the area supported that theory. The four docked vessels were in ruins, their pilothouses riddled with bullet holes and grenade shrapnel. The wood docks were heavily damaged, their planks splintered from what appeared to be grenade explosions.

Thirty yards inland were the two helicopters used by the Red Lightning. They were Mil Mi-24 gunships, supplied by the Russian Air Force. Only a keen eye would pick up on their make and model, for the gunships had been reduced to a shell of their operational selves. Their hulls were blackened and indented with heavy gunfire. The rotors were busted, the cockpit glass imploded, the pilots' charred remains still seated upright. Even after being torched, their killers had made sure to split their skulls with a couple of rifle shots.

Their corpses were not the only ones on scene. Everywhere the team looked, they saw dead strikers laying in the sand. Their attire made it clear that these guys were indeed Red Lightning, and not some opposing group. If anything, the number of bodies implied the island had had a significant security force of at least a couple hundred men. That, or they had received additional troops at some point. Either way, the situation had not played out in their favor.

Whitmore led his men into the warzone. Flies buzzed everywhere, picking at the crispy flesh. Despite the abundance of dead bodies, there was hardly any fresh meat for the bugs to scavenge.

There were at least forty bodies on the beach alone. On the boats were at least ten more, plus the chopper pilots. From what Whitmore could see, every single one had a bullet wound to the head and had been set on fire.

Shell casings decorated the ground. Gray grenade fragments

lined small craters in the sand. One thing was obvious: Whitmore and his men had missed a hell of a party.

"Gerry, Zed, Trent, patrol the perimeter," he said. The three mercenaries hustled to the north and west tree lines in search of any surviving enemy combatants. Whitmore, after gazing at the mass grave, turned his eyes to a radio tower stationed in the clearing between the tree line and the helicopters. "Delta, check the base unit."

Delta quickly made his way to the tower, giving a glance at the chopper remains along the way. On the ground by both gunships were several empty fuel drums.

Whitmore saw them, too, and was able to read between the lines. These helicopters had been intentionally torched, seemingly by the Red Lightning.

Two other fuel drums, as well as several cans of kerosene, were discarded between the bodies. Whitmore picked up the nearest one and peeked through its open cap. As he suspected, it was empty.

Brook approached from the docks. "All four boats are disabled, sir. Control consoles have been shot up. As you can see, they aimed the fifty-cals out to sea."

"Pointed at the other two vessels," Whitmore said.

"Correct," Brook said. "There are casings all over the deck, and a discarded RPG-7V2 on the northernmost one. It appears they were trying to keep these vehicles from departing."

Whitmore inspected a few bullet casings that lay in the sand. "Did you find any NATO-issued casings?"

"Negative, sir. And all weapons are either PP-19 Bizon submachine guns or AK-74 assault rifles," Brook explained. "Most of the gunfire was directed at the boats."

"And those are only the ones we can see. For all we know, there's several others laying on the seabed," Whitmore said. "How many shooters do you estimate?"

"The five that came up from the south and, based on the tracks, at least a dozen more from the west."

Whitmore glanced at the direction from whence they came, then observed the carnage before him. His mind worked to form a mental image of what occurred. Usually, that was easy. Generally, when investigating the aftermath of an armed conflict, he could piece the events together with the evidence left behind. Usually, it was Group A encountered Group B, tempers flared, guns went off. Either one side becomes the clear victor, or both parties depart and lick their wounds.

This one was different. So far, there was no sign of an invading force. If anything, it seemed the strikers stationed here had turned on each other.

"They were firing on their own men," he said.

"Most of it was done by the ones who came in from the west," Brook said. "The fireteam who poisoned the jungle, they didn't appear to have done much shooting. It seems they arrived, then turned northwest with the rest of the unit."

Whitmore thought of the bullet-riddled tree back in the poisoned area of jungle.

"They warned the others," Whitmore said.

"Whatever they were shooting at, none of the unit members were keen on engaging it," Brook added.

"Sergeant Major?" Delta called from the tower. Whitmore approached. "Radio distribution box is disabled. They put a few rounds in it and left in a hurry."

"Can it be repaired?" Whitmore asked.

"With a little rewiring, yeah," Delta said. He grinned. "Why? You hoping to make a long-distance radio call?"

Whitmore did not reward his snarkiness with any signs of amusement.

"I ask because there are still some strikers on this island, and I'd rather they didn't return after we depart and call for backup."

Delta shook his head. "I don't think we have anything to worry about. They clearly did this in a hurry. Deliberately. They don't want any calls sent out, and by the looks of it, they don't plan on returning to this beach."

"Sergeant Major, there's something else you may want to look at," Brook said.

Whitmore followed him to one of the boats. They stepped aboard its aft deck and laid eyes on the dead striker slumped against the transom. Unlike the others, his body wasn't burned. Instead, he was left to rot with a bullet hole in his head and at least five gunshots in the middle of his chest.

Just like the dead boars in the jungle.

Brook directed Whitmore's attention to something even more bizarre. Slumped against the helm was another dead striker, killed apparently by a shot to the head. A pistol lay on the console near his hand, indicating he had committed suicide.

Like the other one, he had not been torched by the unit. What really set him apart was the gaping wound in his neck. It was not a bullet injury or shrapnel wound. A chunk of flesh had been *torn out* from his neck. A bite injury. Not caused by wildlife, but by none other than a human.

Whitmore looked at the dead striker who lay against the transom. Specifically, he studied the dead man's bloody mouth. At first glance, he thought the blood had been coughed up after being shot in the chest. Only now did he realize that blood belonged to the man on the helm.

There was no other way to spin it. The striker had literally bitten his comrade's throat out.

Delta walked alongside the boat and glimpsed the strange aftermath on deck. Right away, he made the connection.

"This guy . . . *bit* this other guy, then was killed by a shot to the head . . . then this guy blows his own brains out . . ."

Twenty minutes ago, Whitmore would have chastised Delta

for the absurd theory he was implying. While he wasn't yet willing to go along with the idea of undead corpses wreaking havoc on this island, he could not deny the strange similarities.

All eyes turned to Lee. The agent had been oddly quiet this whole time, taking photos of the bodies and equipment. Feeling the piercing gazes that were coming his way, he looked to the men on the boat.

"What do you make of this?" Whitmore asked.

Lee joined them aboard the boat, his eyes fluttering at the dead man on the transom.

"Does he have a penetrating wound?"

"See for yourself," Whitmore said, nodding at the gunshots.

"No," Lee said with a strange intensity. "I mean *stab* wounds. Not from a firearm."

Brook flipped the dead man over. "Here, in his back. No powder burns."

Lee gave the injury a glance. The flesh was heavily discolored by infection. The agent clenched his teeth, hissing a single word. "Shit."

"Mind telling us what all this means, agent man?" Delta said.

The look Whitmore got from Lee said it all. *Muzzle your dog, will ya?* It was obvious he had no intention of answering the question, which only sparked more questions in Whitmore's mind.

Why was there infighting within the Red Lightning? How and why did this dead striker get infected? What exactly did it to him? How many others got infected? And, most importantly, why was a U.S. agency so secretive about a foreign enemy's operation—an operation they were eager to destroy?

The breaking of radio silence relieved Lee of the burden of being faced with those questions.

Zed's voice came through their receivers in a ghostly whisper. *"We've got movement."*

Whitmore directed his men back on shore, where they took firing positions.

"Give me a number," he said.

"Single sentry," Zed said.

"Confirm target and eliminate."

"Aye-aye," Zed whispered. He glanced at Gerry, who gently nodded. Both understood the unspoken but most important part. *Quietly.*

They kept low, blending in with the dark green undergrowth as they watched the sentry. It was an odd sight. The man didn't appear to be carrying a rifle. He wasn't unarmed, though. His sidearm was strapped in its holster. A hand radio was clipped to his duty belt. One wrong move, and the striker could have dozens more descending on the mercs.

Gerry and Zed continued to let him walk for a few more paces. There was something stranger than the lack of a rifle. The striker had a slouched posture, his head tilting heavily to the right. Seeing this made the mercenaries reluctant to kill him. Many men had died by their hands, but not a single one unjustly. In their careers, they'd managed to neutralize enemies quietly when they believed killing was not necessary. In this case, there was something clearly wrong with this striker. Perhaps they could quietly capture him and learn what happened at the docks.

Gerry quietly moved to the right, gradually working his way around the target. Now behind him, he began to move in. He drew his knife, closed to within striking distance, then lunged. One hand closed over the striker's mouth, the other pressing the blade to his throat.

"Shhh . . ." he whispered. "One squeak out of you, and I'll make you a Columbian necktie."

Zed moved in and removed the striker's handgun and radio. The striker lashed out with his arms, his posture now straight. Already, it seemed he had no interest in complying, even with an eight-inch blade to his throat.

Gerry could feel the man's lips peeling back, exposing the teeth behind them. He warned him again, and when his order was ignored, he pressed the blade inward and sliced. Blood trickled down the striker's black uniform.

Yet, the bastard kept squirming. Finally, those jaws parted and closed down on Gerry's palm. The mercenary growled in suppressed pain and anger. He freed his hand and pushed the striker away. Still spilling blood from his open throat, the striker turned around, baring teeth, and lunged at Gerry, who knocked him to the ground with a kick to the chest.

Zed drew his own knife and, without hesitation, plunged it through the striker's eye socket. With eight inches of blade in his skull, the snarling soldier finally stiffened.

Zed looked at Gerry. "You all right?"

Gerry removed a piece of gauze from his vest and pressed it to his bleeding hand. "All I can say is I'm not sure I'll listen to my humanitarian side in the future."

Zed lifted his radio to update Whitmore, only to put it away in favor of his weapon. Both men found cover and pointed their guns west. Somewhere behind that jungle was the sound of footsteps and crushed vegetation.

From behind a large shrub emerged a second striker. Like the one they had just killed, he appeared to be in a trance-like state. He had no rifle, his upper body was bent forward, and his jaw was slack. Then there were his eyes. Cloudy. Gray. Lifeless.

Another striker appeared behind him, in exactly the same deathly trance. Behind him, another one emerged. They lumbered along, all at once lost, but at the same time, single-minded in the way they traveled. Like a pack of wolves, they moved toward their dead comrade.

Gerry and Zed exchanged a glance and a nod. *You take the one on the right, I'll take the one on the left, and we'll see who gets the middle one first.*

Both men opened fire, their suppressors muffling the loud cracks of gunshots. Their bullets struck center mass, blowing fist-sized holes in their targets.

The strikers staggered back, their posture straight, their mental status alert. Instead of falling, they quickened their pace, arms outstretched, charging at the suppressed gunfire.

Zed and Gerry adjusted their aim, punching rounds through the skulls of their targets. This time, they fell over. Heads burst, their pink and white contents wetting the surrounding vegetation.

SPLAT!

SPLAT!

SPLAT!

With quick precision and accurate shot placement, the mercs put an end to the assault.

They pressed deeper into the jungle in search of any other hostiles, finally confirming they were once again alone.

"On your nine." From the south emerged Trent, his weapon pointed down as he approached. He squinted at the four dead strikers and the severe bodily damage they suffered. "Was it a 'take a lick'n and keep on tick'n' situation?"

"You can say that," Zed said. He lifted his radio and pressed the transmitter. "Clear. Four hostiles, not one. Area has been checked."

"Any problems?" Whitmore asked.

Zed shrugged before answering. Whitmore had definitely sensed a mild perplexity in his voice.

"It'll be simpler if you just come and see for yourself, sir."

That's exactly what Whitmore did.

Within a few short moments, the sergeant major and the others approached from the dock area. Immediately, their eyes gazed upon the four dead strikers with a sense of confusion and alarm.

"No rifles?" Whitmore asked.

Gerry shook his head. "Just sidearms, and they never bothered slapping leather."

Whitmore raised an eyebrow. "They attacked . . . using close quarter methods?"

"Even that's being generous, sir," Gerry said. "They just came at us."

"Took multiple rounds to the chest before . . ." Zed chuckled, realizing how this would sound. ". . . resorting to headshots."

Delta clicked his tongue, unsure if he wanted to state the obvious comparison. A life-long soldier, he had the patience of an oyster. He had conducted seventy-two-hour stakeouts in the most uncomfortable locations imaginable with no sleep and little food, and always successfully completed the objective. He had stood at post and executed patrols with burns and bug bites eating at his skin, and never once had he complained.

But this was one connection that NEEDED to be stated.

"Zombies," he muttered. He anticipated chastisement from the sergeant major. To his surprise, none came his way. Not from Whitmore or from the other mercenaries.

Once again, all eyes turned to Agent Lee.

"We need to get moving," Lee said.

"Don't act like you don't know what's going on," Whitmore said. "Something's happened on this island . . . something you did not anticipate. The soldiers here had cut themselves off, for chrissake. Killed their own people, disabled their transports, even their communications. Either they were really dedicated to the cause, or they were trying to keep something from getting off this island."

Lee sucked a deep breath through his teeth. Even now, he saw himself as someone above questioning. However, he wasn't stupid. He knew the team would not proceed unless he gave them something.

"Let's get to the lab. I'll take photos, we'll set the charges, and get the hell out of here. If we act fast, we'll be back in the water in an hour or two."

"You suspect we may encounter any more of these guys?" Gerry asked. "Alive or . . . undead?"

Lee stared at Gerry's injured hand. "I, uh . . ." He replayed the question in his mind. "If there are any surviving soldiers, they are probably on the northwest side of the island."

"Should he be worried about that?" Delta asked, pointing at Gerry's hand.

"No . . ." Lee said, breaking eye contact. Three years under-cover, lying every minute, and yet he could not state a single sentence in front of these guys without the truth revealing itself in his tone. "Okay, yes. But it's something we can easily take care of once we're back on the boat."

"If he's got a deadly infection, then I'm not keen on waiting," Whitmore said.

Another sharp inhale. Lee shook his head.

"Sergeant Major . . ."

"Agent, there's no hostages here. Hardly any combatants. You said yourself nobody is aware of this research facility. Unless it's an end-of-the-world situation—"

"It could be," Lee said. The team stood silent, waiting for a follow-up to that statement. Lee groaned. "Listen, this thing, it cannot leave this island. There's a reason the research was being conducted on an island in the middle of nowhere. We can put a stop to it right here and now, but I need to get a look at the lab.

Once we're done, I'll call in an airstrike. But we need to act now."

For once, there was no hint of secrecy in his voice. That was enough for Whitmore. He looked to his team, detecting the same sentiment from them. They were all ready to go and get this job over with.

"Eyes open at all times. Maintain a four-yard spread. Watch for traps." He gripped his weapon and went northwest. "Move out."

5

Psalm 23: 4

Yea, though I walk through the valley of the shadow of death, I will fear no evil . . .

He recited that verse over and over again, but it did little to quell the sick feeling in his gut. Whitmore and his men were indeed in such a valley, one that God never intended to exist.

He was no stranger to gruesome aftermaths. Just two years ago, he and his team patrolled through a mass grave in Burma. Half-buried bodies, left there by the military, gave off a horrid stench that cursed even the hardest of men with nightmares. It was one of many reminders that evil truly existed in the world.

The difference between all those other evils and this one was simple. Those were the result of horrible people doing horrible things. They were motivated by power and greed. They were predictable.

This was not.

For the Red Lightning to cut themselves off from the rest of the world to keep this thing from getting out, such a thing must be death incarnate.

That was Whitmore's gut feeling, and it only got worse as they ventured farther into the jungle.

After a half mile in, the vegetation thickened. Their decreased visibility made it all the more imperative to remain silent. For all they knew, this flora was as much an asset to their target as it was to them.

Two miles in, they found some mild elevation overlooking a small clearing. In the middle of that clearing was the base camp.

Once again, they took in the smell of burnt fuel and flesh. As Whitmore suspected, whatever had happened here, they had missed it. Missed it by less than a day, judging by the thin black smoke rising from the scorched remains of a storage building in the northwest corner.

Whitmore's team dispersed, checking the watchtowers before entering the camp. Zed climbed into the nearest one, immediately looking at Whitmore. He ran his hand across his throat and then flashed his palm, fingers outstretched. It wasn't the number five he was signaling, but rather a horrific, explosive fatality. The guard had been torn to pieces.

The post itself was mostly intact, aside from some thick grooves on the edges. The guard had not met his fate by the explosive power of a hand grenade, but by brute force.

He was just one of many casualties.

With the men in position, Whitmore inspected the camp through a set of binoculars. There was no movement within the camp, with the exception of insects and small birds that gathered over the many stiff corpses. From his current position, Whitmore estimated roughly thirty bodies, many shot and torched, just like those at the dock area.

The mass death, the smell of spent munitions, the burned-down storage building were only a few examples of the chaos that had taken place.

The camp had a pretty standard setup. To the north was the

storage building—what was left of it: the barracks, a few personnel tents, and a mess hall. The buildings were essentially large motor homes, likely airlifted to this destination by helicopter.

On the south end of the base was a larger trailer that probably served as the administration building. To its right was a vehicle shelter, basically a makeshift canopy made with tarp and wood posts. It sheltered nothing, however, for the base's Jeeps were wrecked in various places across the base. One had smashed directly into a tree on the west side.

Two others were wrecked near the barracks, one having plowed through a couple tents before exploding. Only its charred metal frame remained, the rest of its components worn away by hot fire. A fourth Jeep was overturned near the center of the camp, its windshield smashed, its tires deflated, its engine flayed open.

A few yards north of it, standing at the center of the base, was the lab. Larger and more high-tech than the other buildings, it was probably constructed on site. Black siding covered its outer walls. A large generator stood to the east, linked to the lab building by numerous cables. It had endured a lot of use, a fact made evident by the countless fuel drums stored nearby.

The lab had two principal entrances: the main door on the south side, and a secondary door facing the generator. It was the main entrance that had Whitmore's attention—specifically, the damage around it. Bullet holes dotted the building, the highest concentration being around the door frame, and on the interior wall inside the building. The door did not appear to have been forced open, yet the strikers had felt threatened enough to unload on whoever, or whatever, was passing through.

They also had concentrated their gunfire at the top of the building. As Whitmore aimed his glasses at the roof, he made an interesting discovery. A vent covering had been forced open

from inside. It hung by a single screw, its center bulging
outward.

"All teams in position," Trent said through the radio.

Whitmore lowered the binoculars and lifted his radio. "Zed,
Brook, secure the barracks. Gerry, watch the perimeter. Trent,
Delta, Lee, on me."

All at once, they entered the camp. Each mercenary had his
eye looking down the scope or iron sights of his assault weapon.
Rifle muzzles swept the camp in search of a target. So far, all
they found were corpses, burned and shot in the head.

Most of them, at least.

Whitmore and his fireteam secured the admin building
entrance and gazed at the two unfortunate souls who had
perished defending it. One had been run through by some sort
of tipped object. Whatever it was, it was at least ten inches thick
and had a powerful ramming force behind it. There were no
burns or anything else indicative of any ranged weapon. Whatever killed this man had done it up close and personal.

That fact was made obvious by the condition of the second
body. This one had been brutally diced, his legs having been cut
off below the knees, his right arm ripped from the shoulder, his
innards ripped out, and his head severed above the lower jaw.
Edged weapons were used here, which sparked more questions
in Whitmore's mind.

He ascended the three steps and entered the building, Trent
right behind him. They swept the reception area with the
muzzles of their rifles, finding strange impalements in the floor
and walls. These were not bullet hits; in fact, they appeared to
'hook' deeper into the craters. They were in tight groups, with
little sense of structure in their placement aside from the fact
they were leading to a single destination. Or victim.

Whitmore's eyes followed the trail of craters and abrasions
to the far left side of the room. There, another striker had been

violently gutted. His right cheek had been flayed open, hanging off his face by a few strands of skin. His chest had been ripped outward, revealing ruptured lungs and broken rib bones.

Trent drew Whitmore's attention to the wall on the right-hand side of the reception area. The corner near the west hall was marked by three holes. Each one was surrounded by mild scorching from friction and gunpowder. Missed rifle shots, intended for whatever it was that broke in, fired from a room at the end of the east hall.

Whitmore looked at Trent, then tilted his head to the west hall. *You check down there, I'll check down here.*

The men split up, the leader cautiously proceeding into the east hall. He passed the radio room and the commander's dorm, following that weird trail of markings all the way to the commander's office.

The door had been ripped outward piece by piece. Some of those pieces had bullet holes through them. The fella inside had made his last stand here, shooting through his only barricade to fend off his attacker.

Ultimately, it had all proved to be futile.

Whitmore found the commander slumped against the far wall, his pistol on his chest. Before that, it was pointed under his chin, his final shot put through his own brain. Better than being ripped apart. Or infected. Or suffer whatever other God-forsaken secrets this place held.

Whitmore and Trent regrouped in the reception area. Trent cocked his head back toward the conference room and the officers' mess hall.

"No bodies. Some blood in the mess hall. Twelve hours old," he said.

Whitmore nodded, then stepped outside. Lee had already gone to inspect the lab. Delta stood outside its entrance, waiting for his boss before proceeding.

"Anything?" Whitmore asked him.

Delta shook his head. "Just an increasingly frantic agent. I don't know, Sergeant Major. I don't think he expected to find this place like this. Or at least, he *hoped* he wouldn't."

They stepped inside, taking immediate notice of the brownish-red blood smear on the wall. It stretched for nearly ten feet, ending near the corner that led to the main hall. A mental image took form in Whitmore's mind of somebody being lifted, slashed open, and dragged across the check-in room.

They turned the corner on the right-hand side and followed the hall to the laboratory. The power was out, coating them in thick darkness. From deep inside, they could hear dripping water, quick moving footsteps, clacking computer keys, and a distressed voice.

"No, no, no, no, no, no. Good Lord, let this not be real."

Whitmore and his men activated flashlights and entered the lab. To the left was Agent Lee, leaning over one of the lab computers. His own flashlight had been activated and placed on a table, its light shining over the keyboard.

The lab had a cold yet humid feel to it. Eighty-by-sixty feet, it comprised most of the space in the building, the rest being taken up by a small maintenance area in the northeast corner. The remainder of the lab was made up of pieces of advanced equipment, most of which Whitmore could not identify. Whatever they were, they almost appeared futuristic. Huge computer stations with hundreds of buttons and switches were linked to the machines, each one with its own unique purpose and function.

None of this specifically struck Whitmore as odd. It was a so-called research lab. Such facilities would obviously have advanced equipment that only a scientist would recognize. It was the equipment Whitmore *did* recognize that made him do a doubletake.

In the center left of the lab were two holding cells. Thick tubes made of bulletproof glass, they stretched from the floor to the ceiling like pillars. The inside did not give much space for the prisoner to move around, but there was no doubt they were intended for confinement. Near each tube was an IV unit, with a few vials of peculiar-looking fluid in a rack beside them. Hand-prints and scratch marks lined the insides of the tubes.

"Jesus . . ." Trent muttered.

Whitmore turned to the right, seeing the two men aiming their lights at a third holding cell protruding from the east wall. This one was not a narrow tube like the others. It was thirty feet long with three glass walls. The inside was filled with logs, broken branches, and what appeared to be a pond, all of which was covered by a wet syrupy substance.

Delta's light went to the ceiling, settling on a large hole that had been ripped outward.

"Call me crazy, but I don't think it was a person they were keeping in here," he said.

Whitmore focused his light on the glass. Sure enough, the inside was covered with numerous scratch marks. Unlike those in the tubes, these had been caused not by fingernails, but large, rigid instruments.

Leaning in, Whitmore noticed something else on the glass. Spaced ten inches apart were several lines, each one perfectly level, going horizontally down the length of each wall. It reminded him of the grid wires on the back windshield of the Ford F-150 he had in Idaho. Right then, it hit him. These lines were an electrical grid designed to keep the subject from attacking the glass.

His eyes went back up to the ceiling. The thing had torn a path out of its enclosure and opened an exit in the north part of the lab. Under the gap in the ceiling was blood, now dry and discolored. Not a lot, though the floor around it was covered by scratches made by shoe heels. Someone had been forced on his or her back and held in place, leading to kicking and clawing in an effort to free themselves. There was blood near the computer consoles, resulting from a violent clash that smashed some of the instrument panels in the process.

But there were no bodies.

"Sergeant Major?"

Whitmore turned around, finding Delta shining his light on a long wood table on the south side. Two glass containers were placed at its center, surrounded by newspaper clippings, printed articles, and a couple of large sketches.

Both containers seemed to hold some kind of old rock. Holding his light on one, he could see amber-colored layers contrasting with the rock's natural gray. In the middle of it was a worm-like shape.

"It's a fossil," he said.

"Of what?" Delta said.

They turned their eyes to the articles. Some of them had English text regarding paleontological digs in Africa. Some of them had photos of science teams on an excavation site. The triumphant looks on the scientists' faces suggested they had made a major find.

"The hell were they digging for?" Delta questioned, looking at the shape in the rock. "Worms?"

Whitmore put his light on the sketches. They were hand-drawn depictions of what appeared to be an insect. It had a multi-segmented tail, six long, pointed legs, a set of wings that made Whitmore think of a dragonfly, and two large pincers located on large forearms.

On each sheet was a hand-drawn sketch of a human scaled next to the bug. If the estimations were correct, this thing had a body length of ten feet, the tail adding an extra fifteen when outstretched.

Suddenly, the lights came on. Lee, who had been hustling to restore power, jogged to the main computer. He typed in a few codes, granting him access to the mainframe.

"Thank Christ, we're in," he said. He inserted his thumb drive and initiated a download of the major files. "All right, boys. Won't be long before we leave."

Whitmore said nothing. His mind was too busy pondering the government's intention with this research.

Brook's voice came over the radio. *"Sergeant Major, north side is secured. But, sir, there's something here you may want to get a look at."*

"On my way."

Lee perked up upon hearing that exchange. Picking up his gun, he followed the mercenaries out the east door and to the barracks. Brooks was waiting outside, while Zed patrolled the perimeter.

"What is it?" Whitmore asked. Already, he could see that the barracks' entrance had been forced open.

"From what I can make of it, over a dozen men made a stand in here. They barricaded the doors, formed firing lines. There were two forced entries. One through the main door, as you can see. The other through the roof. Some were torn apart. Others . . . best you see for yourself."

As Whitmore neared the entrance, he was hit with a repugnant odor that only rotting bodies could make. Inside, he found battered barricades, severed limbs, a gaping hole in the ceiling, and twelve human corpses on the floor.

They were shrunken, their flesh hugging their skeletons, the skin black, wrinkled, and oily. Yet, their abdominal regions were hyper-extended. Pulsing.

Lee stepped in, took one glance at the bodies, and immediately went out the door. At first, Whitmore thought the agent could not stomach the sight and smell. Then the orders came.

"Get some fuel drums over here. We need to burn these bodies," Lee said.

"What's the matter?" Delta said. "They carrying some kind of infection?"

"Just do it," Lee said. He pulled a SAT phone from his vest and started walking away. "Yes, I need to speak with the General ASAP . . . yes, we'll be needing an airstrike on this place."

Whitmore nodded to Trent and Delta, who went to get one of the fuel drums.

His mind flashed to the big aquarium holding chamber, the articles and sketches, the rotting bodies, and that strange fossil. It sounded too unbelievable to be true, yet he could not deny the things he had seen. It was enough to make him want to wrap this job up quickly and get his team out of here.

Up until now, he'd assumed the Red Lightning had been working on a new chemical weapon. The reality was proving to be much worse.

The Red Lightning had found something—something that Mother Nature herself had deemed too horrible to be allowed to exist. Through her might, she'd buried it with extinction, only for the hubris of Man to dig it back up.

What was once lost had now been found.

6

His eyes opened.

First, there was darkness, then a blinding light as his pupils adjusted. He was on the ground, staring up at the sky, unable to move or speak. A few senses gradually returned. He felt the earth beneath his body, the warm air on his face, the bugs that crawled on his flesh. Next came pain. All kinds of pain. A marathon of pain. A world of pain. Pain that he could not escape. Pain that plagued the short remainder of his existence.

Pain triggered a rush of memories that shocked his fragile mind into function. He remembered his name.

Lijun.

He thought of his military training, his many assignments, his induction into the secret Red Lightning, the arrival on South Fire . . . the containment breach. He remembered running through the jungle with Fabin and Haoxuan, the confrontation that followed, the realization that escape was impossible.

A reality proved by the bug.

Grotesque images and sensations flooded his weak, exhausted mind. From the moment that stinger entered his body, Lijun was reduced to nothing other than a spectator to his own actions. The first few hours were spent in paralysis, all the while experiencing the pains of a growth in his abdomen. Then, the puppeteering began. The toxin in his system had embedded itself in his brain. He remembered walking, though not by his choice. He remembered following the sounds from other strikers and animals in the jungle. He remembered the surprised look from one of his comrades as they came across each other. Then there was the vile taste of flesh and the inability to regurgitate. The being inside needed sustenance, and it was too weak to feed off its host at that point. That would come in about twelve hours.

In those twelve hours, Lijun's body hunted, his mind forced to go along for the ride, providing sustenance for the thing in his belly, and collecting new hosts for the mother to impregnate. In the span of a few short days, the prisoner had become the master, turning its captors into slaves. And when their service was no longer required, they returned to the spawning area, where the cancer-like placenta would break them down.

Most died at some point in this cycle. But Lijun, for whatever reason, did not. His mind held on, despite his eagerness to end it all. Since the moment of being hijacked by the toxins, he had tried to regain control of his body. All he could think to do was will himself into action. Think hard enough. Get those signals from the brain to his limbs. Mainly his right arm, just enough to put his pistol to his temple and squeeze the trigger.

He could smell the rotting bodies of his fellow strikers. The first to be stung, they would give birth to the first batch of the bug's offspring. Though he couldn't see them, Lijun suspected the others were dead. Nobody was designed to live through such a drastic breakdown of their body. Nobody but Lijun, apparently.

The efforts to regain some kind of bodily control continued. It was all he could do at this point. For countless hours, he remained on his back, abdomen throbbing, the parasite shifting. During that time, his efforts seemed futile. Until they didn't.

After thousands of attempts, Lijun was able to turn his head on his own. His muscles strained so hard, it felt as though they would snap the bone. Still, he got a result. Lijun had no delusions of surviving this predicament. Even if he managed to regain full motor function, his body was too badly broken down. All he desired was to put an end to this suffering and avoid what came next. He just needed to get his hand on his sidearm, put it to his head, and fire one shot.

Trying to get his hand to function was like trying to summon some kind of magical power. Little by little, he achieved little grains of success. First, he got his index finger to move, then a couple fingers, then his whole hand. Perhaps the toxin in his brain was wearing off. If Lijun had to guess, he would theorize that the host was not meant to last this long to begin with. For whatever reason, the bug's toxin had it in for him. Or maybe it was just fate. Karma for being involved with an operation that had brought back to life Earth's worst organism.

Lijun did not care why he was alive. All that mattered was ending this misery.

With enough effort, he began to move his arm. His fingertips grazed the dirt and grass, ultimately finding his holster. He scratched at the strap, eventually unclipping it. The effort loosened the muscles enough for them to handle the weight of the loaded firearm. His fingers found the grip. Slowly, he unholstered the weapon. His index finger found its way into the trigger guard. Slowly, gradually, he mustered the strength to angle the weapon at himself.

Head shot, body shot, it didn't matter. As long as the agony was over. As he thought about it, body shots began to sound more appealing. First, it would be easier to angle the gun at his stomach rather than his head. The muscles in his upper arm were still extremely stiff. Second, body shots might also kill that THING moving around inside him.

That thought sparked a tiny, but noticeable wave of pleasure in his mind. At least he would get some kind of payback. The last laugh. After all he had been through, Lijun figured it was the best way to go out.

Lijun angled the pistol toward his stomach and pressed the muzzle against the rotted, bloated flesh. The time was now. Bit by bit, he applied pressure on the trigger.

The occupant shifted. Movement triggered a new wave of unbearable agony that fired up every remaining nerve in his body. Pain quickly led to convulsions, which caused Lijun to unintentionally tilt his gun skyward.

BANG!

The bullet flew uselessly into the canopy. Down below, an awakening took place, shuddering Lijun's body without mercy. A brown foam oozed from his mouth. His teeth clattered as though he was in subzero temperatures.

All the while, he would not die. He wanted so badly to slip away, but his brain refused to switch off.

There was another shift, then immense pressure, both on his back and his front . . . as though something was pushing its way out. His midsection expanded like a mountain of gooey, broken-down flesh. Finally, the meat split, the occupant finally emerging into the world. It extended its long, slimy body from Lijun's stomach, its mandibles yawning open for the first time.

Even *then*, Lijun did not die. All he could do was stare up at the disgusting larva, almost astonished at the fact that its incredible length managed to fit inside him.

It angled its head down at him. The mandibles clicked, dripping slime and saliva. No longer did it require its placenta to absorb sustenance. This was the way of its lifecycle. Once born, it would strengthen its mandibles by feeding on its host.

Lijun gagged, staring at those ugly jaws. The pistol had fallen from his grip. As it turned out, he did not get the last laugh. That satisfaction went to the larva.

It struck in the same manner as a king cobra, sinking its pointed mandibles into Lijun's face.

As fate would have it, he still did not die. It took three more bites, and the complete removal of his head, for that to finally happen.

7

Gerry was patrolling ten yards into the tree line when he heard the gunshot. He found some cover, dropped to one knee, and pointed his rifle northwest.

"Gerry? What do you got?" Whitmore said over the radio.

"One shot, Sergeant Major," Gerry said. "Handgun, by the sound of it. Hundred yards northwest. Want me to scout?"

"Be quiet and careful," Whitmore said. *"Figure out how many guys we're dealing with. Everyone else, form defensive positions. Brook, get up on the lab roof. Good spot to pick the bastards off should they come this way."*

Gerry kept to the shadows, moving swiftly and silently as a ghost. There was good reason to suspect a squad of strikers was on approach. Nobody else could have fired that shot. It was likely they had seen the barracks fire, which produced a big plume of black smoke. Perhaps they had encountered an infected human, mad with disease or a mind virus or whatever the hell was being produced in that lab.

The thought of infections did the impossible. It made Gerry extremely nervous. His hand ached where the nutjob striker had bitten him, the flesh around the wound discolored. The veins in his arm were turning purple. At best, he was facing some kind of blood infection. It that's what it was, Gerry would shrug it off. At least he would understand what he was dealing with and would know what medications to get his hands on. But he was bitten by what almost appeared to be a walking corpse. Who knows what disease or bacteria that guy was carrying? The last thing he wanted was to lose control of his mind and body. Sure, Lee had said something about having an antidote on the Navy ship, but who could trust a word that jackass had to say?

He pushed these concerns from his mind in favor of focusing on the task at hand. So far, he had not heard anything else after that gunshot. No movement, no whispering, nothing. Almost nothing. Somewhere behind that vegetation was the buzzing of insect wings. This was not one or two flies. This was a damn swarm. Taking in the cruel odor coming from that direction, Gerry was suddenly no longer worried about strikers being in the area. His hand ached more, reminding him of the encounter near the docks. Not just reminding him but warning him of what might be waiting behind that undergrowth up ahead.

Finger on the trigger, Gerry emerged in a small clearing. It was as though he had stepped into a deep chasm where many unfortunate lifeforms had fallen to their doom and were left to rot. Everywhere he looked, there were thin, bloated, twisted corpses strewn about. Men, animals, all in a horrid state of decay. The ground where they lay had turned black, the vegetation dying as though a dark plague had swept through the area.

That wasn't the worst, or even the most bizarre, aspect. Gerry turned his eyes twenty feet ahead on the left of the clearing. For a moment, he genuinely wondered if his infection had caused some kind of hallucination, because what he was looking at was too freakishly horrid to be real.

But real it was, complete with its own putrid odor that was somehow even worse and more distinguishable than that of the corpses. Its flesh was pinkish-white and leathery, covered in thick translucent slime. Its shape was narrow and elongated. A worm . . .

Gerry noticed how its tail end was still embedded in the abdomen of a human host.

A LARVA.

Now the condition of the bodies made much more sense. They had become food for these . . . *things*.

Its head was burrowing into the skull of its host. Off to the side was the dead striker's outstretched arm, a pistol mere inches from its grasp.

The guy had been alive long enough to experience the birth.

In a whip-like motion, the larva raised its head. Its pincer-shaped mandibles, like those on a trap-jaw ant, yawned open, dripping blood and skin tissue.

Gerry took aim at the creature. Its body's width was roughly equal to that of a man's bicep. Not a hard shot. All he needed to do was focus his aim for a moment . . .

The creature hissed. There was a mass of white suddenly plastered all over Gerry's midsection. A moment later, he was yanked to the ground. Facedown in the muck, he was pulled toward the hissing worm.

"Christ!"

He reached for his rifle. The worm retracted its silk rope, pulling him from the reach of his dropped weapon. Cursing, he pulled his knife from its sheath and tried to cut away at the silk.

The larva ejected the silk strand in favor of a newer, thicker one. A wet sticky white mess crossed the near twenty-foot distance and struck Gerry, many of its strands catching his right arm. Once again, it pulled, using short, thin digits located under those mandibles. Like the legs of a spitting spider, it steadily retracted the web, bringing its victim ever closer.

His arm now seized by the substance, Gerry could not go for

his sidearm. His body slid against globs of mud and grime, completely at the mercy of this creature.

And there was no question that this creature had no concept of mercy, let alone intention. It was a born killer, hard-wired for nothing other than slaughter. With its secret weapon, it had already gotten the better of this hardened veteran.

Gerry was left with only one option. He grabbed his radio from his vest and shouted into the transmitter.

"GET YOUR ASSES OVER HERE ON THE DOUBLE, GODDAMMIT!!"

THE TONE in Gerry's voice said it all. The mercenaries did not waste time with questions. They dispersed from their defensive positions and followed Whitmore's lead into the jungle.

"Delta, go left. Trent, right."

"Sergeant Major . . ." Lee began.

Whitmore knew what he was about to say and was already fed up.

"One word out of you about holding back, and I'll see to it that you'll join those guys in the barracks."

Lee had the utmost confidence that Whitmore was not kidding. With that in mind, he bit his tongue and followed the team into the jungle.

As the team pressed onward, they heard the sound of struggle. A fierce odor entered their nostrils—an odor that was becoming all too familiar to them.

They emerged at the clearing. Whitmore's gut feeling proved to be right. It was another mass grave, containing strikers and animals alike. Everything in here was decayed beyond identification. Everything except Gerry.

There he was, face-down in the mud, feet kicking as he was

pulled toward a monstrosity that could only have been sculpted by the devil himself.

Delta emerged from the jungle, immediately alarmed at the freakish sight. "What the fuck is that?"

As bizarre and mind-boggling as this creature was, it was not hard to identify. It was a gigantic larva, armed with razor-sharp mandibles and projectile silk. Its lower half was coiled inside the body of a striker, its upper half fixated on tearing into Gerry.

The mercenary raised his head to the sound of Delta's voice. "The hell are you pricks waiting for? Shoot the damn thing, will ya?!"

Whitmore centered the creature in his iron sights and squeezed the trigger.

The larvae's head kicked back, detaching the web strand. Green blood and white flesh jetted from its neck where the bullet passed through. Snarling, it angled its jaws at the new arrivals. Whitmore fired several more shots, forming a near perfect line of bullet holes down the creature's body.

The larva writhed in place, its insides spewing from its many wounds. Like blowing out a match, the life left its body. It fell to the left of its host, its upper half coiling into a single loop.

The team converged, with Brook and Zed rushing to Gerry's aid. Using knives, they gradually managed to detach the silk rope from his vest and arm.

"I think it's obvious why Agent Lee was determined to barbecue those bodies in the barracks," Delta said.

"Damn straight," Lee said. His straightforwardness was almost as unexpected as the sight of a twelve-foot worm. The cat was out of the bag. The contractors had seen the thing. All he cared about at this point was keeping them from seeing any more. It was not a matter of secrecy, but survival. "We need to move. We need to . . ."

A wet sound that simultaneously resembled stretching and

squishing caught his attention . . . right before a wet, sticky substance splattered all over his back. Before he knew what hit him, Lee was yanked backward. Now on his back, he was scraping the mud, straight toward the jaws of another larvae.

Freshly birthed from its host, it was ready to make its first kill. Drooling saliva and dripping fluid from its neck, it used its little digits to reel the agent closer.

Whitmore and Trent went into action, gunning the larva down in a violent display of rifle fire. Hissing in agony, the larva squirmed. Whitmore was not taking any chances. Tilting his muzzle up a few degrees, he fired a shot through its head. The larva fell to the ground, its victim quickly scampering to his feet.

His relief was overshadowed by the sight of over a dozen other corpses throbbing. Their abdomens stretched, the skin splitting and peeling outward like flower petals. One after another, the larvae rose several feet high and stretched their jaws. Sensing the fresh meat nearby, their killer instincts kicked in.

Delta swallowed, his eyes wide. "Holy . . ."

"Weapons free," Whitmore said. He initiated the conflict by putting nearly a dozen rounds into the nearest worm. Spurting blood, slime, and innards, it collapsed, its life over as quickly as it began.

Gerry was the next to open fire, eager to get some payback for the sins of their brethren. His rifle shots tore into their target, shredding the wet rubbery flesh.

A strand of projectile webbing found Zed. The merc had no intention of being yanked off his feet. He located the offending worm and dotted its neck with bullet holes. The creature hit the ground, its tiny legs coiled around the silk rope.

Lee took part in the action, shredding one of the worms as it attempted to flee its host. Emptying half his magazine into the thing, he left no margin for error. The bastard was dead as a doornail.

A few feet past it were two other bodies, their torsos shifting as the parasites threatened to awaken. He put several rounds in them, guaranteeing the larvae they housed would never see the light of day.

"Do not let any of them escape," he said. "Our mission is now containment."

Zed and Trent stood shoulder-to-shoulder, baring teeth as three worms slithered at them, ready to get up close and personal. Multiple explosive impacts put an end to the nearest one, then the next. The second larva danced like an Egyptian cobra, its head pointing skyward while its body spat its insides through numerous wounds.

The third managed to close the distance. Zed and Trent cursed, moving in separate directions. The larva went after Trent, its body mass stretching to nearly thirteen feet. Feeling the creature's presence closing behind him, Trent spun on his heel, his Beretta M9 drawn and pointed. He managed to squeeze off two shots before the creature sprang. Its head and neck struck him, driving him to the ground while the rest of its length constricted him like a boa.

Now on his back, Trent could do nothing except put his pistol to the larva's seemingly eyeless face.

BANG! BANG! BANG! BANG! BANG! BANG! BANG! BANG!

The slide locked back, all seventeen rounds now inside the worm's brain. Trent exhaled, glad to have been able to keep those mandibles from tearing into his face.

The squelching of mud made him look to his left. "Aw, fuck."

A larva was coming right at him, its dead brethren having done most of the hard work. Even in death, it kept Trent pinned and restrained. He shifted, determined to grab ahold of one of his spare magazines. The larva came within three feet, cocked its head back and expanded its jaws, ready to strike.

BANG! BANG! BANG! BANG!

The larva reeled backwards, its body twisting and contorting into a demented series of shapes. Whitmore and Brook stepped closer, the former putting three more rounds into the invertebrate, bringing its squirming to an end.

Behind them, Zed and Delta proceeded to gun down another one. The only thing rivaling the deafening cracks of gunfire was Delta's cursing, as one of the worms had managed to hit him with silk in an attempt to immobilize him.

As quickly as it began, the nest had gone silent. The mercs reloaded and checked the area, ultimately confirming all hostiles were dead.

Lee went from corpse to corpse, placing several bullets in each one. Meanwhile, Whitmore helped Trent to his feet. The mercenary kicked the dead larva that had nearly bested him, then reloaded his weapons.

"You all right?" Whitmore asked, half grinning.

"Better than all those poor fuckers," Trent said, pointing the muzzle of his rifle at the bodies.

They watched as the agent put another few rounds into the bloated abdomen of a host. Suddenly, the bullet holes they'd found in the boars and unburned bodies made total sense.

"Secure the area," Whitmore said. "Perform some abortions, and then we'll get the hell out of here."

8

"What do you think, Sergeant?" Lieutenant Qin Guang asked.

Sergeant Seto Zixin looked in the direction of gunfire. The conflict was a few hundred yards away, the vegetation preventing them from getting a visual of what was taking place. Regardless, just the echoes provided enough intel for the sergeant to have a good idea what was going on.

Behind him were three dozen strikers, the last Red Lightning force on the island. It was unlikely another response team had dropped in, for they would have heard the choppers on approach. Plus, this was definitely a small squad, judging by the number of firearms that were going off.

Seto's keen ear picked up the most important detail. Between the bursts of gunfire were the sounds of voices. They spoke English, which meant only one thing: a foreign paramilitary unit had arrived on the island, likely working for the United States. This sparked two new problems. The first was the revealing of the secret operation taking place on this island to the rest of the world. Though run by an 'independent organization,' it would potentially put international scrutiny on the motherland. Not only that, but if these westerners somehow managed to be successful, they could potentially steal the data to be used by NATO or some other organization.

The other problem was contamination. Should these intruders end up infected, this could lead to the specimen and her horde getting off the island. Her sting did more than provide a host for her offspring. It created another loyal servant, utilizing not only their body, but certain aspects of their mind. All she needed was for just ONE of them to alert reinforcements . . . to bring a transport to the island . . . to provide new hosts and slaves.

"I'm thinking the same thing you are," Seto said to Qin. "We need to move in and eliminate them while we have the chance."

Lieutenant Qin kept his eyes to the northeast. Every few seconds, there was another quick burst of gunfire. Aside from that, the intense chaotic clash seemed to have come to an end. With no other strikers on the island, that left the question of *what* exactly the westerners were shooting at. The bug? The horde? Or something else?

"What's the horde's last known location?" Qin asked.

The sergeant laid out a paper map. He pointed out their current location, then ran his finger northeast.

"Based on our last encounter, probably less than a mile this way."

"They'll probably be moving in the direction of the gunshots," Qin said. "We can hit the intruders, then use our explosives to lay out a trap. Two birds, one stone."

"Yes, sir," Seto said.

One of the strikers inched closer to the team leaders. "Sirs? What about . . . the big one?"

"That's not what they're fighting," Seto said. "Even if it was, we'd still have to make a move. We can't risk these bastards getting off the island. Alive, or otherwise."

He shouldered his AK-74 and rose from the dark cover

provided by the canopy. His pants and gear were decorated with mud and moisture, souvenirs from hiding in the jungle for days.

Qin stood up and turned to his men. The three dozen strikers rose to their feet, ready to sneak through the jungle and surprise the new arrivals. After the disaster that had wrecked their initial objective, at least they would experience the satisfaction of taking down an enemy fireteam.

Qin let Seto lead the way. Slowly and quietly, they advanced on the enemy's location.

"SERGEANT MAJOR, you might want to take a look at this."

Whitmore turned to face Brook, who was kneeling by a human corpse he had just shot. He approached and knelt by the dead man's head, where Brook was pointing.

"What am I looking at?" Whitmore asked.

"Front teeth," Brook said. "That's flesh."

It was not often that Whitmore winced, but sure enough, the idea of cannibalism managed to do it today. And there was no doubt that was human flesh caked between this person's teeth. The tiny piece of black fabric removed all doubt. Its victim was undeniably human.

Equally as strange was the secretion coming from the gums. It was a swampy green color, thicker than saliva, clearly teeming with bacteria. At first, Whitmore thought it to be part of the digestive breakdown of the body, which clearly was being used to nourish the larva inside. Yet, there was no such secretion anywhere else on the body. Only the jawline, the stuff sticking to the teeth as though by design.

He thought of the dead man on the helm of the gunboat back at the docks. That man had not only been bitten. He had been *infected*. Forced to blow his own brains out before succumbing to the toxic effects of the disease.

He looked over at Gerry. The mercenary was patrolling the west side of the nest, brushing some of the mud and residue off his pants. It was only a matter of time before he started showing symptoms. Based on everything he had seen up to this point, Whitmore did not believe Gerry had much time left.

Whitmore opened his mouth to order the team to withdraw, only for the sound of gunfire to silence him.

"Got some over here!" Delta said. He was shooting past the tree line where some other hosts lay, perfectly hidden in some undergrowth. Whitmore and Brook rushed over to him, just in time to see the aftermath of his gunshots. Two corpses, both ready to birth, were now deflated, the slimy occupants inside put to death.

"Check the perimeter," Whitmore said. "Make sure we don't have any more stragglers."

Gerry found one and put a few rounds in it. A few yards to his left, Trent and Zed found and executed one.

"Hold up!" Lee said. The team went silent, everyone listening intently.

They all heard it, that vile wet sound of tissue stretching to the breaking point.

Trent and Zed moved a few yards westward.

"Contact!" Zed exclaimed. There was a hiss, then a rush of motion, followed by gunfire.

Whitmore ran in their direction, catching a quick glimpse of the pinkish-white worm as it darted southwest into the jungle. Trent's shots went wide, hitting vegetation instead of flesh.

"Damn it, it's fast," Trent said.

Lee, weapon pointed, was the first to pursue it into the jungle. "Come on. We can't let it escape!"

Whitmore shook his head. He wasn't fond of this idea, but there was no time to argue about it. In addition, he did not like the idea of patrolling through the vegetation with that thing out there possibly stalking them.

"Brook, you and I are up front. The rest of you maintain a five-yard spread and follow us. Keep your eyes peeled."

Brook took point, tracking the larva's slimy trail. Agent Lee stepped aside, allowing the tracker to take the lead. He gave Whitmore a nod, simultaneously thanking him and conveying the message that this matter could not wait, that it needed to be addressed immediately.

Whitmore did not question that fact, at least not for now. Once they got off this damn island, he vowed to reconsider working with the agency ever again. If today's events had taught him anything, it was that some jobs were simply not worth it.

Those were decisions for later. For now, he had a big ass worm to kill.

SERGEANT SETO RAISED his fist and crouched, his men taking cover. The gunfire had suddenly increased. There was a sound of movement coming straight in their direction.

"Eyes open . . . Looks like they might be coming toward us . . ." He took aim at some swaying shrubs a few yards straight ahead. He put his finger on the trigger and tensed, ready to blow the brains out of the American intruders.

The shrubs bent down, pushed by a large narrow mass. Seto raised an eyebrow. This was something he had not yet seen. The moment it took to identify his target proved to be his downfall, for the larva had no trouble identifying its target.

Springing off its tail end, it tackled him to the ground, its body wrapping around him as though it was the arm of a monstrous kraken. Seto yelled, his gunshots flying into the air. His strikers moved from cover, ready to shoot at the thing, but hesitant, for Seto would certainly be killed in the process.

The worm absolved them of that consequence. Its jaws plunged into Seto's neck, resulting in a fountain of blood and the sharp cracking of bone. In that same moment, Seto's head rolled clear of his body, the worm raising its bloody face at the strikers ahead.

Shrieking, Lieutenant Qin opened fire on the thing. The creature reeled backward, hissing maniacally as it squirmed. Globs of flesh burst, erupting its bodily contents.

As he caught his breath, he was alerted to a new threat, the very one he and his team had intended on ambushing.

Looking right back at him was a tall American man, holding an M16A2 with an underbarrel grenade launcher. The only thing worse than that was the pissed-off look on his face, for this man was definitely one of vast experience, and knew exactly what these strikers had in mind for him and his team.

The following moment brought a puff of smoke from the grenade launcher, the whistle of a projectile narrowly missing Qin's head, and the shockwave of an explosion several yards behind him. Three of his men were launched through the air, their bodies coming apart as they went.

Ears ringing from the grenade blast, Qin could only manage to bellow one order.

"Kill them!"

THE LARVA's escape turned out to be a blessing in disguise for Whitmore and his team. It had slithered directly to its own doom, and in the process, revealed the threat which had been zeroing in on their location.

Whitmore's first action was successful, his grenade putting

an end to three strikers. He moved to the side, firing numerous bullets into the enemy platoon.

"Party time, boys," he said. "Trent, Zed, circle around to the west, keep them from escaping that way. Delta, Gerry, go east. Watch your crossfire. Brook, as usual, you're with me. Lee . . . do whatever the hell you want. Just keep your sorry ass alive. Might not get paid otherwise."

He, Brook, and Lee provided cover fire while the rest of the team moved into position. After a few seconds of spraying bullets, the three men dispersed, blending into their surroundings while evading return fire.

Several strikers, not having seen the other four mercenaries, began moving in on Whitmore's position. From the jungle came another grenade, which launched another three of them into the air. The others backpedaled and went for cover, the platoon branching out to prevent golden opportunities for explosives.

Their methods only served to help Whitmore further. He moved from tree to tree, scattering the enemy gunfire while his team identified the targets.

Brook, with pinpoint accuracy, detected two strikers crouched to Whitmore's ten o'clock. Using his carbine, he punched warm gaping holes in their chests, knocking them backward.

Whitmore identified another target and struck with a three-round burst. A few enemy bullets whizzed by, the shooters struggling to pinpoint his exact position. Brook was able to get a visual. He took down the first with a few well-placed shots, while Agent Lee took down the other.

Whitmore moved again, successfully gunning down another target as he neared another tree. Whitmore swiftly moved around the trunk, slamming the butt of his rifle into the striker who had intended on ambushing him. The striker fell to the ground, his rifle still in his grasp. He aimed it toward Whitmore's head, only for the mercenary to beat him to the punch. Or gunshot, to be more precise.

After punching a hole in the striker's forehead, Whitmore turned his gun on a small group taking position up ahead. The platoon was falling back to assume better tactical formation. Lee and Brook were laying down suppressing fire from his left, both frequently pressing toward the enemy position.

Then came more gunfire from the east and west. The Red Lightning was gradually depleted in personnel, the strikers overwhelmed by the accuracy of Whitmore's team.

Trent and Zed moved in from the west, killing several strikers with grenades. Rifle shots followed, forcing the enemy back toward the center of the kill zone.

Gerry and Delta hit them from the east. Gerry, using his natural gift of stealth, managed to sneak up behind a striker whose attention was on Brook and Lee. This time, when his knife slid across the man's throat, Gerry felt the desired result. Letting his kill drop to the ground, Gerry approached another. This striker sensed him at the last moment and turned around to shoot, only to end up with Gerry's blade through his neck.

Delta did not bother with close-up tactics. He was too busy gunning down enemy personnel and watching their numbers rapidly dwindle. He moved left, firing in three-round bursts, grinning after seeing the pink clouds burst from his targets.

More grenade explosions threw the strikers into more disarray. It seemed that no matter what they did, they could not land a single blow on the smaller enemy squad. Many of them dug into defensive positions, while others went north in hopes of flushing out the team's commander.

It was exactly what Whitmore wanted.

He emerged from cover, blasting holes in one of the strikers.

The others returned fire, missing him as he moved to the right. As Whitmore arrived at his next spot, he found a clear line of sight at a group of strikers digging in behind a fallen tree, exchanging gunfire with Zed and Trent.

Never one to miss an opportunity to put his grenade launcher to use, Whitmore fired a shot into the enemy location. The resulting blast tore one of the strikers to shreds while throwing the other two for several feet.

"Damn it, boss!" Trent exclaimed. "Ya stole my kill. Bastard."

Whitmore would have smirked at that had it not been for the sound of footsteps coming up behind him. He spun on his heel, spotting three strikers who were still determined to flush him out.

A burst of gunfire took down the nearest one. The other two advanced, guns blazing. Whitmore ducked to the side, his magazine empty. With no time to reload, he drew his Desert Eagle, popping the skull of the next striker as he came around the tree.

The other one held back, opting to use a grenade instead. The pin fell free, the metal ball full of shrapnel bouncing just a few feet shy of Whitmore.

He dove for cover, the resulting blast rippling through the earth. Whitmore ended up on his back, the Desert Eagle having slipped from his grasp.

The striker approached in search of what he hoped to be a kill. To his surprise, he did not find Whitmore laying in pieces. When he did finally see Whitmore, it was when he sprang from the jungle with the speed of a leopard.

Whitmore knocked the enemy's gun muzzle to the side and struck the soldier with an elbow to the face. He yanked the gun free, drove his opponent back with a kick to the chest, and shot him with his own weapon.

He turned the rifle muzzle southward, ready to take down

any remaining targets. The sound of gunfire was diminishing, the mercenaries having successfully closed in on the kill zone.

"We got some runners," Brook said. "Three men retreating south."

Whitmore tossed the AK-74 aside and located his M16A2 and Desert Eagle. "Anyone hurt?"

"Only my ego," Zed said. "You were hogging them all."

"Well, if you were a better shot, you would have killed more of them," Whitmore replied.

Zed snickered. It was exactly the kind of thing he expected his boss to say.

"What's next?" Gerry asked.

Whitmore looked in the direction the three remaining strikers retreated. Same as with the larvae, he did not like the thought of leaving a confirmed threat on the island, knowing they could set up an ambush during the team's return trip to the southeast shore.

"Your hand doing okay, Gerry? Feeling all right? You're looking a little flushed."

"I'll be fine," Gerry said.

"We can't leave those men out there," Lee said.

"Why?" Delta said. "Because they saw us? That's half the reason you hired us. Plausible deniability, right, Mister Agent?"

"Because they saw *me*," Lee said. "The lieutenant in charge of this group, I worked with him while I was undercover. If he manages to get off this island or get a call out, that'll be bad for our country diplomatically."

"Oh, fabulous!" Delta exclaimed.

"Another reason I don't like people piggybacking," Whitmore muttered. Groaning, he looked at Gerry. "Sure you'll make it?"

"Three assholes left," Gerry said. "With Brook tracking them, it should be easy work."

"All right then." Whitmore looked at Brook and tilted his head southwest.

The tracker got right to work, immediately finding the strikers' trail.

Into the jungle they went, ready to finish this job and get the hell off this island.

9

It was a disaster. A complete and total disaster. This entire operation, whose executive officers had adamantly claimed to be foolproof, had become a catastrophe beyond comprehension. And yet, despite the mistakes of those in charge, despite false promises to the president, despite warnings from the science staff, the blame would inevitably be cast on the Red Lightning.

Lieutenant Qin wondered if there was any point in attempting to escape from this island alive. He was a man second in command of an operation worth billions of U.S. dollars. He was in charge of over a hundred men, twice that after the reinforcements arrived. After all the planning, the training, and extra manpower, he had been down to thirty-six men.

Now, he was down to two. He had lost almost all his remaining forces and failed to inflict even a single casualty on the seven-man infiltration unit.

All he had left was Private Ning and Private Zhu. Arguably the two biggest cowards in the entire unit. They were loyal and well-meaning . . . until it came time to get their hands dirty. How these men managed to get selected into the Red Lightning, Qin would never know. To be fair, their cowardice had

probably worked in their favor today. Their comrades, men
who were eager to fight and kill, had been decimated by the
enemy. It was only through pure luck that Qin had gotten out
of there in one piece. If given the choice, he would rather
wander through this jungle with these two cowards than on
his own.

Not that it made much difference. The transports were gone,
the radio tower disabled, the containment units wiped out. It
wasn't as if there was a way off this island. And they certainly
weren't alone.

The three strikers came to a stop. Qin found a rotten tree log
to sit on and catch his breath. Ning and Zhu kept their eyes to
the east, watching out for the Americans. Both men repeatedly
glanced in his direction, waiting for some kind of guidance.

Qin, though he would not admit it out loud, had no answers.
His mind was lost in a state of limbo. Stress led to indecision,
and with it, the realization of how much Lieutenant Qin had
relied on Sergeant Seto's intuition. Without him, Qin was lost.
Every option felt like a bad one. In a sense, they were. Seto
would have acknowledged that and gone with the least-bad
option.

Moreover, he would know what that least-bad option was.
Qin went over every available course of action in his mind. Set a
trap for the Americans; return to the docks and repair the radio
tower; try and fix one of the boats; dig in and wait. Which one
was the least bad? Even if they escaped, Qin would have to face
the wrath of his superiors, who would undoubtedly blame him
for his failure in containing the specimen. Digging in would be
prolonging the inevitable. Compared to what lurked in that
jungle, a firing squad sounded preferable.

"What now?" Zhu asked. "What do we do?"

Qin stood and switched out his partially spent magazine for
a fresh one. His body language alone made the two cowardly

soldiers uneasy. Ning was already backing away, his eyes shifting between the Lieutenant and the direction of the Americans.

"It's suicide to go after them," he said.

"Every option is suicide," Qin replied. "But if we manage to kill those scum, maybe the regime will look favorably on us for preventing the West from obtaining our nation's secrets. Maybe we won't be doomed to execution when we get off this rock."

"Lieutenant, it's hopeless," Zhu said. "You saw what happened. We won't last five seconds against them."

"Things would have played out differently had they gone according to plan," Qin said. "We would have killed those men before they had a chance to get a shot off. But that . . . thing . . ." His voice trailed off. "That thing . . . the specimen is replicating itself. If any of them manage to make it offshore, our problems are only just beginning."

"So, what do we do?" Ning said, taking another few steps back. The 'flight' response was kicking in hard, putting the striker near to the point of retreating into the jungle and taking his chances alone.

"Don't even think about it, striker," Qin said. "If you bolt, I'll empty this rifle in your gut. I'll make sure you feel each bullet. I mean it. Choose carefully, Private."

The terrified Ning held completely still, his weapon held at port arms. His eyes remained on the lieutenant's rifle, fearing its muzzle would swing in his direction. There was no doubt in his mind that Qin was dead serious.

Zhu approached Qin. Though nervous, he maintained better control of his wits than his comrade.

"You want to set a trap for the Americans? How? Odds are they're coming this way as we speak. They're bound to have a tracker who can scope us out. We don't have time to make an elaborate setup. Every footstep we make will be clear as day."

"It's our only chance," Qin said.

"You're gonna get us killed!" Ning exclaimed, jetting spit with each word.

"You devoted your very souls to the Red Lightning when you were selected," Qin said. "Stop your bellyaching, you blubbering cowards!"

"Call me what you want, sir. As long as I'm alive," Zhu said. "I don't see the point in dying uselessly like our men did. For no gain."

Qin pivoted, giving Zhu his full attention with a borderline demonic glare.

"I figured you for a coward, but not a traitor. What would you do? Surrender to the westerners?" Qin felt his blood boil after the private broke eye contact. "You sick piece of filth. You actually would. Why, you pathetic excuse for a soldier." He tilted his rifle muzzle in Zhu's direction. "I ought to shoot you right now—"

BANG!

The rifle fell from his grasp. Qin stumbled backward, seeing the smoke coming from Ning's gun muzzle. He looked down at the gaping hole in his abdomen. His insides burned and inflamed, the nerves in his spinal column firing signals from where the bullet had lodged. Qin fell to his knees, his hands clutched over the wound to keep his guts from falling out. Ning stepped forward, shocked by what he'd just done. There even a hint of regret, for the soldier had crossed the Rubicon. With this action, he was officially a traitor to the Red Lightning and its mother nation.

Qin spat blood, waiting for the coward to finish him off. The only thing that hurt more than his guts was his pride, for his demise had come at the hands of a squeamish, jittery idiot. Qin could not think of a worse way to go out. He wanted to draw his pistol and give what he had gotten, but the pain had him in a paralyzing grip. All he could do was sit on his knees and suffer this dishonorable fate.

Ning, accepting the fact that he must follow this deed through, took position in front of the Lieutenant. The will to live trumped all things, including his oath to his nation. He took a shaky breath and took aim at Qin's head.

BANG! BANG! BANG! BANG! BANG!

Gasping, Ning turned toward the sound of Zhu's crackling rifle. The striker had been knocked to the ground, his gun firing into the trees. Panting and clawing at the dirt, Zhu was pulled into the jungle. In an instant, he was fully obscured by the thick plant life.

Ning heard a scream, then a grunt, then silence. His rifle shook along with the hands that held it. He turned his head to and fro, up and down, jumping at the slightest sounds. Every rustling of leaves, scraping of dirt, and brushing of wind carried an aura of peril.

The thing was out there. Somewhere. Everywhere and nowhere all at once. Its hesitation was part of its tactic. The victim was getting clumsier by the second. Fright flooded every sense. All it took was the slightest sound to get his attention.

Qin gagged, his blood pressure taking a plunge.

Ning, misinterpreting the sound as either fear or the pain from being attacked, spun toward the lieutenant, ready to blast away. Qin gagged again, only this time it was out of fright. Not from seeing the striker pointing the gun, but from seeing the grotesque being emerging from the jungle behind him.

Arching backward, Ning let out a deflated gasp, feeling every inch of the razor-sharp appendage in his back. His muscles stiffened, no longer in his control. In the blink of an eye, he was a shell of his former self, the only genuine trait being the look of utter panic on his face.

The creature let his body hit the ground, then moved over

toward Qin. Studying the wound in his lower torso, it immediately knew this human was not suitable for impregnation. That did not mean he could not be useful, however. A beast its size needed to eat, after all.

Qin stared the specimen in the eye. His personal disgust at being killed by a traitor was gone. Now, he desperately wished Ning had finished him off.

The lieutenant hollered as his wound was widened and his guts were extracted by a flurry of claws and mandibles.

Slurping entrails, the bug raised its head. It could sense others in the area, slowly approaching its location. These humans were worse than its captors. They had already murdered many of its offspring, as well as several potential hosts. They were a fiercer breed, one that needed to be handled with stealth and caution. Fortunately, the bug had many tools at its disposal.

Expelling a faint chemical signal, it ascended into the canopy. There, it would wait.

10

Whitmore kept his breathing shallow and his eyes trained on the jungle ahead of him. It had been at least four minutes since they heard the gunshots. First it had been a single discharge, then after several moments, an automatic burst, all from an AK-74.

The team members rested in position, taking advantage of the relative peace and quiet. Between the recent gunfight, the constant trekking, and the humidity, they were experiencing the first pangs of fatigue. Being professionals, they only needed a few moments of rest to recharge their batteries.

Lee was the only exception. The longer they remained in place, the more antsy he became.

"You know, Agent, the more you fidget, the more you give away our position," Whitmore said.

"The longer you make us wait here, the more distance those men put between us," Lee replied.

"Something tells me we won't have to worry about them anymore," Whitmore said. "Either they turned on each other, or they encountered something. Based on what we've seen here on this island, my money's on the latter."

"We have to confirm one way or another," Lee said. "That officer saw my face. If he manages to get word out . . ."

"They wrecked their own communications equipment," Whitmore said. "Their boats have been shot up. Most importantly, they're on an island which, for all we know, is crawling with worm monsters. They're not going anywhere. My men, on the other hand, do have a way off this rock, and I think it's time for them to use it. We've placed the charges in and around the lab. You've downloaded the files you needed. This was not part of the agreement."

A toothy snarl came over Lee's face, like a rat in a cage who was ready to bite the hand that was about to reach in and grab it. Like that hypothetical rat, he was outmatched, but was more than willing to fuck up Whitmore's day regardless.

"If you want your men to get picked up by the chopper, you will complete the task," he said. "One call on my SAT phone will see to it you never leave this island."

Whitmore turned his eyes toward the agent, his gaze expressing a hundred different thoughts, none of which were friendly. Lee already had the code dialed, his thumb on the call button, the receiver to his ear. It had become perfectly clear at this point that the only way to win this argument was to shoot the prick. Such an action opened up a can of worms all by itself. It would give away their position and alert the strikers, or whatever was out there, to their position. That, and the reality of killing an active C.I.A. agent, was a no-win situation. If the team made it back intact, but without Lee, and more importantly, the data, they would be disappeared.

Whitmore did not like backing down to Lee, but once again, it was the simplest solution given the circumstances. He nodded, which proved to satisfy Lee, who put the phone away and repositioned his weapon.

Giving hand signals to his men, Whitmore advanced. Delta and Gerry swung left to flank the enemy, Brook and Zed taking the right. Like the tip of an arrow, Whitmore took the lead, Trent and Lee ready to provide backup at a moment's notice.

After moving for fifty yards, Whitmore heard Brook give off a bird-like whistle. He made his way to the tracker's position, finding him and Zed eyeing a patch of trees to the west. Between those trees were two bodies on the ground.

"Looks like you were right about those strikers not going anywhere, Sergeant Major," Brook whispered.

Whitmore glanced at Lee, then back at the bodies. "Gee, who would've guessed?"

"Can't tell for sure if the third one is deceased," Zed said. "If he's present, he's obstructed by the flora."

"I can assure you, *something's* present," Whitmore said. Shaking his head, he stepped forward. "Let's secure the area, identify the bodies, and bug out. As long as the lieutenant is dead, our liaison will quit bitching." He could practically feel Lee's blood pressure rise after hearing that statement.

All seven men converged on the bodies. Gerry, Zed, and Trent monitored the perimeter while Whitmore, Brook, and Lee examined their findings.

It was the lieutenant all right, what was left of him. His final moments were not ones to be envied. His abdomen had been torn open, its contents mashed and sprawled out onto the grass. After the events at the nest, it did not take much imagination to figure out what had happened here.

"We've got problems, Sergeant Major," Brook said.

Whitmore nodded and looked at the other body. Unlike the lieutenant, this soldier's body was perfectly intact. He was face-down with a single penetrating wound in his back. Whitmore had flashbacks to the bodies on the boat.

He looked into the canopy. "We're not alone."

Lee stood over the striker and put his gun muzzle to the wound. Several bullets entered the body, then one to the head. Now, the striker was truly dead.

"Could've handled that in a quieter way," Delta growled.

"Doesn't matter," Whitmore said. He watched Brook examine the ground. The soil was marked with a series of pointed tracks, placed in a similar manner as those on the interior walls of the administration building. They led to the nearest tree, whose trunk was also heavily marked.

Naturally, their weapons pointed to the canopy. It was not a worm that intercepted these men, but something far worse.

"Gerry, Trent, Zed, return to our location," Whitmore said. "I want everyone in sight."

"Roger that. But, sir," Gerry replied through the radio. *"We've got movement out here. No visual, but I hear something. Multiple bogeys, coming from the north and west."*

The three men quickly returned, each one taking firing position. Zed and Trent monitored the west, ready to blast anything that moved.

Whitmore's attention was on the north. Listening intently, he picked up the distant sound of approaching footsteps. These sounds were undoubtedly human, though they lacked the caution that a trained unit should have. These were lumbering movements, lacking any sense of stealth or caution.

"Hold your fire unless necessary," Whitmore whispered. "Try and get a visual."

The team waited silently.

That silence was suddenly compromised by Gerry's abrupt coughing. The mercenary backed away, his hand pressed to his mouth in a desperate attempt to suppress his own gagging. His eyes were bloodshot, his normally dark skin now ghostly pale.

"Gerry?" Delta whispered. "Get it together, man."

Gerry put one hand up. *I'm good, I'm good.* Except he wasn't good. There was no fighting back against this new sudden onset of symptoms. He bent forward and vomited. Even then, he tried to feign the appearance of being fine. That façade ended with his loss of balance and the seizure that followed.

"Christ!" Whitmore pointed to Delta and Lee. "Help him. Everyone else, keep your eyes peeled. Brook, do you have a visual?"

Brook peeked to the north. "Got three, all wearing Red Lightning attire. They're not carrying weapons."

Delta knelt by Gerry. The seizure reached its conclusion, leaving the merc lying stiff on the ground.

"Gerry? Gerry! Shit!" He checked for a pulse.

"Damn it," Lee muttered. "Thought we had more time."

Delta looked at him. "Time until what?"

Lee pointed his rifle. "Get away from him."

"Whoa, whoa . . ." Delta responded in kind, putting himself in a stand-off with the agent. "Don't even think about it."

"Did you get a pulse?" Lee whispered.

"I can revive him, but you need to focus on what's out there," Delta said.

Lee shook his head. "There's nothing we can do. For god's sake, get away from—"

They heard a sudden wheeze vibrate from Gerry's throat. Delta put a finger to his neck, smiling with relief.

"Wait . . . got a pulse. It's faint, but—"

Gerry sprang up, eyes and jaw wide, his arms extending toward his brother-in-arms.

Cursing, Delta thrust his rifle into Gerry's chest, blocking his demented attempts to *bite* into him. His eyes were pale and riddled with red blood vessels, his teeth and gums excreting some kind of strange fluid.

"Holy goddamn!" Delta exclaimed.

Lee stepped in and put his muzzle to Gerry's head.

Zed, seeing this, put a hand out in protest. "Wait!"

Gerry's skull split open, the gunshot echoing into the jungle. The noise from the wandering strikers intensified. Drawn by the noise, they converged on the team's location.

"Incoming," Whitmore said. "Weapons free."

"Head shots," Lee said. "Take head shots."

They emerged from the jungle, absorbing the blockade of bullets as they lashed out at the mercenaries. Whitmore was immediately forced backward, his target on pace with him, having taken two rounds in the chest. Shifting his barrel upward, he hit the fiend in the forehead, killing it.

It was the proper term for these so-called men. Though they looked human, they acted like wild animals. They were feral, driven by a mad instinct to devour raw flesh.

They were fast, having identified their prey and committed to pursuit. Some of the slower ones were scrawny, their flesh discolored from the offspring residing inside of them. Regardless, they were functional enough to hunt new prey.

For every one Whitmore killed, two more seemed to show up. They had no strategy except numbers and brute force. It was a tactic designed in an age prior to firearms and military maneuvers. Even that struggled to fend off the overwhelming force.

Trent and Zed, popping off rounds with quick precision, were forced backward. Even Brook had to break formation. This enemy was essentially a flood, a force of nature that moved with destructive force, causing chaos.

That chaos caused separation, the team members forced to move in different directions while keeping the drones off their backs.

Whitmore and Lee moved southeast, a frenzied group of six on their tails. Lee fired off a few shots, hitting one of them in the head. The others took grazing hits to their shoulders, their fast movements making headshots difficult.

"Watch out," Whitmore said. He aimed low, spraying bullets into the thighs and hips of his pursuers. Muscle and bone broke apart, unable to perform their functions. Like dominoes, the drones hit the ground. There was no indication of pain or self-pity, nor was there a desire to give up. Crawling on the ground, they remained determined to bite into the mercenaries.

Whitmore and Lee executed the five drones, then listened to the sounds of rifle fire. Brook was a few yards west of them, having managed to get onto some high ground. It was an area rich with undergrowth and rocks, which served him well by tripping up the clumsy drones.

"Heads up, Brook, we're coming in from the east," Whitmore said. He and Lee closed in, finding Brook on the branch of a tree, gunning down his attackers. Lee and Whitmore joined in, rupturing skulls while their attention was on the tracker.

One by one, they dropped, gushing blood, brains, and other vile fluid, which definitely was not originally part of the human body.

"Where are the others?" Whitmore asked.

"We're scattered all over the place," Brook said. He hopped down from the branch and reloaded his weapon.

Two more drones emerged from the jungle, snarling, reaching at them with bent fingers. Whitmore gave them a devastating greeting, popping their heads open like ripe fruit.

Brook lifted his chin, analyzing the directions of the other mercs' gunshots.

"Got someone over this way," he pointed northwest, "and someone that way." He pointed east.

"Bastards got us all over the place," Whitmore said. "All right, Lee and I will head this way. Brook, help out whoever's over there." He tilted his head at the sound of gunfire in the east.

"On it." Brook took off, vanishing behind multiple layers of vegetation.

In this moment of isolation, Whitmore had half a mind to put the muzzle of his weapon to Lee's temple. *Nobody would know.* For better or worse, he was a killer, but not a murderer. Plus, there were more pressing concerns at hand.

The two men raced northwest. Once this situation was resolved, Whitmore would set his sights on the agent.

"Damn! Crazy zombie sons of bitches," Delta grunted, carving the chest of an oncoming drone. The man-thing was knocked backward by the force of the bullet hits, the mouth now bubbling with blood and grime.

Another one stepped over its still-writhing body, baring teeth. Delta split its head with a three-round burst.

As another one approached, Delta was forced to sling his rifle and draw his sidearm. The first shot went low, splintering the drone's jaw. It arched backward, blood free-flowing down its neck and chest. Without any hint of pain or fear—except for the bloodshot eyes—it turned toward him. Even as its lower jaw hung by a few strands of tissue, it was still determined to bite into him.

Delta put the reanimated striker out of its misery, the back of its head bursting as the bullet made its exit. Confirming no others were coming at him, he stood over the writhing drone. It was unable to stand, despite its desire to grab ahold of him. For once, Delta found himself feeling sorry for the lost soul inside. These guys were not evil by nature. They were the victims of a system that saw them only as cannon fodder. Now, they suffered a fate worse than death.

Delta fired, the striker's misery now over. He panned the gun left and right, in search of any other drones. None were present.

Delta took a deep breath and relaxed his shoulders. He was alone.

So he assumed.

The brushing of leaves overhead was faint. A less trained mind would not have picked up on it at all. A well-trained mind would pick up on it TOO LATE.

Delta looked up. Gasping, he aimed his pistol at the mass of arachnoid legs and claws. Razor sharp pincers closed over his arms, sparking pain. His finger closed over the trigger, not defensively, but automatically as his nerves lit up.

The creature hardly noticed the gunshots. With hardly any effort, it hoisted Delta into the canopy. A stabbing pain made him freeze. Almost literally. In the blink of an eye, his body failed to respond to his brain's commands.

He was paralyzed, a prisoner to this horrid fiend. He could not flee or call out. All he had was his mind and sense of touch, a mercy at first, a curse when faced with the realization of having no escape from this living death.

The first sensation was of being dragged through the trees.

Brook arrived at the location of the gunshots. There were multiple drones lying dead on the ground. No team member. Observing the tracks, Brook moved near a tree, finding a dropped Beretta M9, its slide locked back. There was no other sign of movement from this spot. Not one single track. No blood. No sign of struggle.

"Sergeant Major? What's your status?"

"Wrapping things up," Whitmore replied. *"We've got Trent and Zed over here. I'm assuming you've found Delta? He all right?"*

Brook gazed at the pistol, the tracks, and the tree. "Unknown, sir. He's not here."

It was driving him mad. Looking at where the tracks dead-ended, it seemed as though Delta had vanished into thin air. Dematerialized.

He looked to the canopy.

Or had been lifted straight up.

11

With his rifle run dry, Whitmore switched to his Desert Eagle. With one shot, he killed the last of a dozen drones that had Zed and Trent pinned. The two men were on the far side of a creek, the thick flora working both in their favor and against it. After running into an area with impassable jungle, they were forced to speedily forge a makeshift barricade out of vines and broken branches.

"That does it," Zed said, stepping over the dead drones. "This was not a coincidence, running into this horde. Can't be. I'm not buying into the idea they were simply wandering nearby. No, my 'spidey sense' is tingling. Something's up."

"Hold that thought," Whitmore said. He lifted his radio. "Brook, you find Delta yet?"

"Negative, sir."

"All right, stand by. We're coming to you." Whitmore tucked his radio away. "Damn it."

Their attention turned to Lee. He was on his SAT phone, nodding along with whoever the hell was on the other end of the line.

"Correct . . . correct . . . right . . . data has been retrieved; charges are set. What's the word on the airstrike? . . . Mmm, that's what I was afraid of . . . Okay, but know the situation is hot. We're looking at a possible Inferno-level scenario . . . What about the Philippine or Vietnamese militaries? One of them could probably bomb this place and maybe avoid a diplomatic crisis . . . I see. Okay, we'll finish things up here. I'll set the beacon off when we near the extraction point."

The agent spoke as though he was a corporate rep reporting to his CEO about the week's sales. There was not even a hint of acknowledgement about the recent incident. Certainly none whatsoever about Gerry's death, or the fact Delta was missing.

Lee turned to face Whitmore. "Well done, gentlemen." He pulled a detonator from his vest and extended its antenna. He pressed the button, triggering the explosives at the lab. The resulting explosion was both heard and felt. Before long, they would see its smoke trail high in the sky.

"So, that's it then?" Zed asked.

"Correct," Lee replied. "Time to get out of here and get you paid." He noticed Whitmore scoffing. "What?"

"Not what he meant," Whitmore said. He glanced at Trent and nodded. Lee was grabbed from behind and placed in a chokehold. Cursing, he tried to wrestle his way out of it, failing to outmuscle the mercenary. Zed unsheathed his knife, and with a scowl on his face, put the blade to Lee's groin.

That ended the struggle.

Teeth clenched, Lee stared past the mercenary at the team leader. "You're making a grave mistake."

"The grave mistake was letting you dupe me into taking this job," Whitmore said. "One of my men is dead, another missing. You lied to me about Gerry's condition."

"I didn't lie, I just . . . AGH!" He winced, feeling Zed's blade press against his manhood. "I was wrong about the rate of progression. Had I known, I would have suggested he extract with his diving gear. A chopper would have picked him up. I swear."

"What the hell is going on out here?" Whitmore said. "What happened to him? What happened to all of these men? What were they doing on this island, and what is the agency's involvement? And I swear, if I hear the words top secret or plausible deniability or any other bullshit like that, I'm giving Zed the green light to turn you into a woman."

Lee glanced at the knife, then at its handler. There was no doubt these men would follow through on their threat. He'd always believed himself to be devoted to the agency. Hell, he had spent three years undercover with the Red Lightning. Then again, he'd never considered undergoing slow, painful mutilation in service of his country. Most of the sacrifice related to his service was paid for by other people. Assault teams, like the one he was currently with.

It was at this moment Lee found out who he truly was.

"All right! All right!" He felt the blade ease off his manhood. He took a moment for his heart rate to slow down, then endured the humiliating process of spilling the beans. "You saw the lab. You saw the nests. Those worms . . . larvae . . . they were the offspring of a genetic experiment. A specimen, an insectoid creature that our scientists believe existed in the Mesozoic Era."

"You're telling us a dinosaur bug did all this?" Zed said.

"Yes," Lee said. "We didn't know it was loose. That made getting the computer data all the more important, because one way or another, this island's getting bombed to hell."

"How many are there?" Whitmore said.

"At the moment? Just one," Lee said. "If any of its larvae manage to survive, that'll change."

"You mean to tell me that this one creature injected all of those bodies with eggs?" Trent said.

"Just one of them is capable of producing thousands of larvae," Lee said. "How long does gestation last? This is our first real study of it, so to speak. Probably two days. Probably varies with the host or the egg."

"And how do you explain *The Walking Dead*?" Zed asked.

"Its stinger carries a form of toxin. It infects the brain and essentially puts the victim under a form of hypnosis. They spend their first several hours in service of both the specimen and the embryo within them, providing sustenance and securing new hosts to be infected and impregnated. Their jaws secrete the toxin, meaning anything they bite soon falls under the specimen's control. That's what happened to your man, I'm sorry to say."

Receiving a nod from his boss, Trent let the agent free. Lee instinctively felt himself, assuring his mind that everything was intact.

"The hosts, are they still alive after the toxin takes hold?" Trent asked.

Lee nodded. "We believe so. Most die when the larva begins to feed off their bodies, which starts after a day or so."

"You said they serve the specimen," Whitmore said. "How does that work?"

Lee shrugged. "Possibly chemical signals."

"Wait," Zed said. "That horde that attacked us, you mean to say they were SENT?!"

Whitmore thought of the markings on the tree where they found the dead strikers. He looked up, studying the trees with dreaded anticipation.

"Shit. It's here." He grabbed his radio. "Brook, you there?"

"Yes, sir."

"Still no sign of Delta?"

"Negative."

"Okay. Hang tight. We're coming to you. Keep your eyes peeled and stay away from the trees. There's something worse out there."

12

It remained deathly still, making itself one with the tree, unseen by the lone human that lurked below. The diversion had proved successful, but at great cost. The entire herd of carriers was dead, as well as the offspring within them. These humans were by far more dangerous than the others. So far, its exoskeleton had been able to withstand the smaller weapons they carried on their thighs, but their larger primary weapons appeared to pack more of a punch.

The human had his eyes on the trees, as though it sensed its presence. There was a sound of sniffing, that nose picking up faint traces of the bug's chemical odor. No doubt, this human was an integral part of the pack, possibly more so than the others. Eliminating this one would severely weaken the pack.

It remained in place, waiting for the human to let his guard down. Just a few moments was all it needed to spring down and sting this victim.

That window of opportunity never came, the probability now zero. From the west came the others. They gathered around the spot where it had abducted the other of their group.

Perplexed at the nature in which their member had disappeared, they were on guard.

If the bug had learned anything about this species, it was that there was always a way to outsmart them. Even the more specialized ones such as this group always had a chink in the armor. Two of them were already neutralized, proving this fact.

Soon enough, maybe even in the next couple of minutes, another opportunity would present itself. For now, the creature waited and observed.

WHITMORE'S GUT compressed at the sight of the dropped Beretta and the empty cartridges around it. And there was no doubt the weapon had been dropped and not discarded purposefully.

"How far out did you search?" he asked Brook.

"Sixty-yard radius," Brook said. "Nothing. No tracks, no shell casings, nothing."

Whitmore walked over to the numerous bodies that had been put down by Delta prior to his disappearance. Most of the bullet hits were from his carbine, a few others appearing to be nine-millimeter. Yet, the gun, which held a magazine with seventeen rounds, was empty. He could not buy into the idea that Delta missed most of his shots. Especially not against these targets.

He returned to the gun and stared straight up. Squinting, he spotted a marking in the branch of the tree. A bullet crater, matching the size of a nine-millimeter.

"It got him."

"Come on, Sergeant Major," Zed said. "We don't know that." That sentiment ended after he saw the bullet hole in the tree branch. It was precisely above where Delta had been standing.

"That bastard. It swooped down and grabbed him. Brook, how the hell did you, of all people, not notice this?"

Brook did not answer. He stood a few feet north of the pistol, sniffing and watching the canopy. His rifle was pointed at a thick batch of leaves. The others could not see anything, but they trusted their tracker's intuition.

"Listen, men," Lee said. "I know I'm the last person you want to hear from, but facts are facts. We need to evac."

"Yeah?" Zed said. "You seemed to be in an awfully big hurry to have us kill the larvae and your ol' buddy the lieutenant. You mean to tell me you don't want us to hunt and kill this thing?"

"Because we won't win," Lee said. "It's smart. It used the horde to separate us, isolate us. That's how it got Delta. It won't face us head on. It knows better."

"We can't leave," Whitmore said, his eyes and gun muzzle focused on the tree.

Lee shook his head and groaned. "Why? You initiating some personal vendetta against the thing? Getting revenge for your men?"

"There's that," Whitmore said. "But more precisely, this thing won't let us leave. If we move to the torch, it'll track us. Pick us off one by one. We need a game plan, or else we'll never make it to the beach."

Lee exhaled through clenched teeth. Though he did not want to admit it, he knew Whitmore was right. Also, there was no way he would win any argument with these men at this point. His authority was as meaningful as a white crayon.

The five of them moved slowly south. Whitmore looked around, finding an area of elevation that would serve them well as a defensive position.

"We'll set up over there. Vegetation and canopy are fairly sparse. The thing will have a tricky time getting close to us unseen. Set up claymores and flares. Lee, get your map out. I want to know the safest way to the torch."

IT REMAINED PERFECTLY STILL, watching the men as they moved away. They were onto it now, a fact made clear by how they looked at the trees. It was unconcerned, for time was on its side. The creature required little sleep, unlike the humans it stalked. Sooner or later, it would have its opportunity. Either through stalking them one at a time, or all at once in a bloody battle, the creature would avenge its species.

13

Before long, the high ground was surrounded by flares, claymores, and other flammables. The team was thorough in securing their defensive position, leaving zero room for that thing out there to sneak in undetected. Even the trees were marked with trip wires and explosives.

Now came the time to wait, rest, and plan.

It was Trent's turn to get a quick snooze. Despite having a genetically engineered prehistoric monstrosity hunting him, engaging in three violent firefights, and losing two of his teammates, he was out as soon as his eyes closed. That was part of their training: rest your body and senses, regardless of the environment and situation.

Brook stood guard on the east end of camp, Zed taking the west. Every fern, twig, blade of grass, even the breeze was monitored. All five men felt a sixth sense alerting them of something perched in the jungle, watching them.

"All right," Lee said, laying out a physical map. "We're here, the lab's up here, our gear is here." He ran his finger along various parts of the island, ultimately settling on the torch. He shook his head and sighed. "I don't know what to tell you,

Sergeant Major. You want a clear path to the extraction zone, but as you can see, none exists."

"Then our best bet is to head straight east until we hit the shoreline," Whitmore said. "We can move south from there with decent visibility."

"Maybe, but I'm not sure it'll be as simple as that," Lee said. "If we are where I think we are, we've got some obstructions in our path. We go east, we'll likely run into some mud pits adjacent to a large freshwater pond. It's like the La Brea tar pits. You get stuck, you've basically added yourself to the fossil record."

"We'll have to hook around then," Whitmore said.

"Pretty much go back the way we came," Lee added. He folded the map and tucked it away. He watched the jungle, keeping Whitmore in his peripheral vision. The mercenary's disdain for him was subtle, but displayed on his face, nonetheless. "You might not think it right now, but you and your men have done a good thing."

"Did we now?"

"Yes," Lee said. "Had you not come here, these larvae would have birthed freely. Maybe would have gotten off the island."

"Aren't your bosses trying to arrange an airstrike?" Whitmore said. "Those worms and the infected would have died in that."

"Supposedly, unless they can swim," Lee said. "There have been fossilized remains found in coastal areas. They may even possess the ability to grow wings and fly."

"Can the specimen fly?" Whitmore said, his brow furrowed.

"Not anymore," Lee said. "The scientists surgically removed its wings once it metamorphosed. But they noted characteristics in its bodily structure even before it cocooned itself. It's possible, being contained in a large aquarium and all, it didn't sprout wings fully until it became an adult."

Whitmore turned away, back to monitoring their surroundings. He didn't want to look at the agent any longer than he had to. The attempt to somehow justify the deaths of his men acted as fuel for an already blazing hot fire within him. There was always risk with these jobs, but Gerry's and Delta's fates had been preventable. They didn't die trying to storm the island or take the lab. No, they found themselves cleaning up after the C.I.A.'s mess. And there was no doubt the agency was as much involved as the Red Lightning.

"You seem to know a lot about what went on in this lab," he said.

"I was undercover for three years," Lee replied.

"Don't bullshit me," Whitmore said. "There's a reason the agency sent us here now. Let me guess: you had another person on the inside. Probably a lab worker. Am I right?"

Lee tried to think of a convincing lie, only to come to the conclusion that none existed.

"We were receiving encrypted updates, informing us of the progress. That's how I know the effects of its sting, how its toxins affect the host, the growth rate of the offspring. You saw the holding chambers in the lab. They were experimenting on human subjects."

"Don't try and paint the Red Lightning as a bunch of dirty fiends as though the agency has no blood on its hands," Whitmore said. "There's a reason you wanted that lab destroyed and the computer files downloaded. The Red Lightning was designing the thing as a weapon. The C.I.A. wanted it for the same purpose. The fact you all are so eager to erase all trace goes to tell me you guys were involved in the creating of this thing. Maybe funneling money to this group to provide financing, using 'independent third parties.' Then, after the enemy develops this thing, you all get to ride in and steal it under the guise of saving the day."

Lee could not help but smile at that. Whitmore was no dumb brute. He knew how the game was played.

"And you're so virtuous?" he said. "How many coverups have your team taken part in? How many weapons and data and personnel have you retrieved that ultimately led to greater amounts of death somewhere in the world? And for what? Oh, wait, I already know. Money. Funny, only when you or your team is affected do you suddenly care. War is a business, Sergeant Major. Business breeds competition. It's an unfortunate reality, but a reality all the same. If we don't compete, the other side will proliferate out of control. It's a cold war of sorts, with a few hot sparks here and there."

Whitmore said nothing. What could he say? As much as it stung to acknowledge it, even in the privacy of his own mind, Whitmore could not refute the truth. He'd spent his whole life working for the machine, on active duty and in the private sector. He was the best at his craft, forged by years of the best training and medicine the military had to offer. A specimen.

The silence was overtaken by the burning hiss of a bright red flare. All heads turned to the northwest. Trent jumped to his feet, fully alert as though he had slept for eight hours in a five-star hotel. Weapons were shouldered and pointed, fingers on the triggers.

"Up there," Zen said, pointing to a large tree.

Whitmore watched the flare arch in the sky, its trail touching the top branches of a fishtail palm tree. Its vegetation was thick, exactly why they felt the need to plant trip wires there.

Brook stepped beside Whitmore, his unblinking eyes studying every square inch of that tree.

"Movement. Midlevel."

"You sure?" Trent said.

Whitmore wasn't in the mood for waiting games. Tilting his grenade launcher upward, he launched the small explosive into the canopy.

The resulting blast shook the massive plant to its core,

cracking some of the branches and shaking loose much of its green garments.

A crackling sound followed as something large hit one of those weakened branches in freefall. There was another crunching impact, then the THUD of a heavy mass hitting the ground.

What Whitmore saw was a chaotic flailing of black legs and a segmented, serpentine tail reminiscent of modern-day scorpions.

No order was given, nor was it needed. All at once, the men blasted away. Bits of flora spat through the air like confetti as high-caliber projectiles tore through the jungle.

Through the ear-pounding gunfire came a high-pitched hiss. The thing righted itself, tripping another flare as it darted into the jungle.

In that split-second, visual contact was lost. The men still fired off rounds in the creature's trajectory in hopes of landing a lucky hit.

Silence took over. The air stiffened, as though Mother Nature herself was terrified of incurring the wrath of the mercenaries and their new enemy.

After several moments, Whitmore slowly advanced on the spot where the thing had fallen. Brook was right behind him, Zed and Trent keeping back to provide cover.

The ground had been torn up, the shrubs shredded and uprooted by razor sharp projectiles. The two men stopped to check their surroundings, not keen on potentially getting ambushed. As far as they could tell, the coast was clear.

"Down here, Sergeant Major," Brook said. He knelt in the center of the ravaged ground, dipping his fingers into a yellow fluid. "Blood."

"And some chippings from its shell," Whitmore said, picking up a small semi-circular fragment off the ground. Detached from the rest of the body, it resembled the glass from a broken beer bottle.

"Doesn't look like we did much more damage than that," Brook said. "The son of a bitch has a durable exoskeleton, sir. I know damn well I hit it a lot more than this."

"At least we know we can hurt it," Whitmore said. "Better yet, *it* knows we can hurt it. That's why it won't engage us head on. It's smart enough to know it won't get through the fight unscathed."

"Who knows?" Zed said, shrugging. "Maybe it's saying to hell with it and is taking a hike. Not all prey is worth the effort, right?"

The red-hot flare shooting high from the east side of the perimeter served as an answer to his question. The team regrouped and raced to the location, getting a quick glimpse of the vegetation shaking as the specimen tore through.

The team fired off a few bursts in its direction. It was not a tactic they could use repeatedly. Ammo was limited. Judging by this creature's size, agility, and ferocity, there was no hope of defeating it without high-caliber weapons.

Whitmore watched the flare fizzle out. Though he was glad it had served its purpose, it also infested him with a sense of dread. This thing absolutely WAS NOT going away. It viewed them as a valuable prize, which it had no intention of letting go.

There was no leaving this area without the specimen on their heels.

"Any ideas, Agent?" Whitmore said.

"No," Lee said. "This thing's only ever been observed in a controlled setting. It's like it knows what it's doing. Like, it's toying with us. Letting us know we can't leave."

"Our tax dollars at work," Zed muttered.

Whitmore loaded another grenade into the underbarrel.

"For the meantime, we wait. Who knows? Maybe we can figure out a way of setting a trap. It's smart, but it can be fooled."

"Yeah?" Lee said, smirking. He did not find the situation funny, but rather was absorbing the reality that his sins were coming back to haunt him. Never in a million years could he have anticipated the thought of sharing the same fate as the people in those holding chambers. "Just know, that thing is planning, too. God only knows what other tricks it has up its sleeve."

14

He awoke.

At least, he believed he was awake. He was somewhere dark and murky, his body stiff as a board, forced to endure the annoying and sometimes prickly feeling of bugs and spiders scurrying over his body. Despite retaining control over his mind for the most part, he had trouble piecing together the details of his situation.

He was lying face-up in a deep section of the jungle, that much he knew for certain. How long he had been here—that he did not know. Mentally, he felt as though he was stuck in a void where time did not exist. The throbbing headache did not help. That, or the dull pain in his back.

Focusing on that pain, he triggered a memory. Gunfire, bodies hitting the ground, movement overhead, and the pain of edged appendages seizing him and lifting him into the tree. There was the jolt of a pointed object penetrating his back and the sudden paralysis that followed. Everything after that was a montage of images as he was carried and dragged into the depths of the jungle. For the first time in many years, he was truly afraid.

That fear spiked to levels he did not know were possible as the next chain of events commenced. First, his neurons lit up, confirming to his mind he was awake. Though conscious, he was stuck in a nightmare.

He began to stand up, even though he made no conscious effort. It was a slow, clumsy process which he had no control over. After rising to his feet, he looked back and forth. Again, there was no conscious effort. It was as if his body had become its own entity, leaving him merely as a spectator to his own actions.

There was a vile taste in his mouth and the feeling of an oily substance coating his teeth. His arms began to move against his will. His right foot moved forward, completing a step. His left foot was next, leading him to an unknown destination. The effort to command his body proved useless. An invisible puppeteer had taken control. All he could do was go along for the ride.

A mild odor filled his nostrils. Whatever it was, it was not from the jungle. It felt almost chemical in nature. That sentiment was reinforced by the sudden flood of memories. It wasn't the memories specifically, but his brain's sudden fixation on them that made him certain this was a chemically induced experience.

First, he thought of his name: Walter Manes. His life scrolled before his very eyes like a movie, each image coming and going. It all moved in fast-forward motion, everything: his first time at the movie theater, Christmas celebrations, swimming at a lake with friends, school, graduation, his first kiss, his first lay, his decision to enter the military.

It was here the memories became clear and precise. His nickname echoed in his brain—Delta. Another montage of senses and images swept past his mind's eye. There was basic training, every instance he fired a weapon. The montage came to a bizarre pause. Next thing he knew, he was hyper-aware of the fact that he had no firearm. His pistol was dropped during his abduction, his rifle lost somewhere during the time he was dragged through the jungle. All he had were grenades.

As soon as that realization came to mind, his brain combed through every single experience he'd ever had with the small explosives. First, there was his initial training. His trainer went through all the details on how grenades worked and how to use them. Then came his first time throwing one. Then every instance using them in combat.

Not only was there a focus on every instance he'd used grenades, but also on everyone else in his life who'd used them. Friends *and* enemies. In one such instance, he had been part of a firefight supporting the Afghan National Army against Taliban terrorists. One of the enemy fighters, with no regard for his own life, rushed an Afghan gunner's position with two grenades in hand. BOOM. He was gone, his target of five men dead or in disarray.

Right then, the memories stopped. In that same moment, Delta's body turned southwards and started walking. He had no clue where he was going, but he knew whatever was in control of him had a horrid intent.

He tried to resist the movements but could not. He tried to bite his tongue and bleed himself out, but he could not. He tried to black out, to spare his conscious self of whatever his body was about to do, but he could not. He tried to scream, but he could not.

All he could do was witness this trek through the jungle. Before long, he came across some familiar landmarks. There was the tree and the dead enemy combatants. He turned east, eventually finding the tree where he had been abducted by that thing. That insectoid thing, black as hell, hanging from its tail, reaching for him.

Delta had never considered himself a good practitioner of faith, but he still considered himself a believer. One thing he reminded himself was that God was incapable of making mistakes. Yet, this creature could not possibly be part of His creation. It was too evil. Thus, he concluded that this creature was not a product of God, but the devil himself.

His body turned southeast and stumbled to an area with fairly high elevation. It was surrounded by thick canopy, the rising itself relatively open. It was then Delta realized his puppeteer's plan.

Another chemical signal entered his brain, prompting his next action.

Again, Delta tried to scream. He could not.

"You have a way of thinking on your feet, don't you?" Agent Lee said.

Whitmore and Brook were on their knees, inspecting the trunk of a tree on the east end of their camp. Growing from its bark were several silvery-gray fruiting bodies. Hoof fungus, shaped literally like a horse's hoof, was plentiful in this area. It was the fungus' other name—and use—that interested Whitmore. Tinder fungus, used as early as 3000 BC, lived up to its name.

"It's the best option we have," Whitmore said. "The thing will keep toying with us until we make a mistake or run out of ammo. We need to switch up our tactics."

"By cooking it?" Lee said. His humor was lost on the others.

"This stuff burns easy. We use this and some of that ornamental grass Brook found, we can set a few traps. Lure the thing in, light a trail of gunpowder, bathe the fucker in a sea of fire."

Lee stepped past him and knelt by a pile of grass the mercenaries had torn from the earth. It was fairly dry, making it applicable for producing a bonfire quickly. As the agent continued inspecting the area, he took notice of an odd orange growth protruding from the ground.

"What's this?"

"Ah! Ah! Ah!" Brook leaned over and slapped Lee's hand away from the stuff. "Unless you want to get some inflammation and an infection, I recommend not touching that."

"The hell is it?" Lee said.

"Poison fire coral," Whitmore said. "Highly toxic fungus. Looks like a bunch of carrots growing out of the ground like that, but don't be fooled. Those are no veggies. Those things will kill you in a day."

Lee pulled his hand back. "Good to know, even though I'm not dumb enough to eat anything out of this jungle."

"Dumb enough to touch it, though," Brook said. "The toxins can be absorbed through the skin. It'll act even faster if exposed to an open wound."

Lee looked at the splinters in his fingertips. On their own, they were merely a nuisance. But out here, those tiny gaps in the skin could easily mean life or death.

"Okay! Good to know." He moved away from the fungus and helped Whitmore scrape shavings of the hoof fungus from the tree. For a minute or two, they worked in silence. Meanwhile, Trent was on watch while Zed got some shuteye. Hating the dead silence, Lee decided to attempt some small talk. "So . . . has anyone actually been dumb enough to eat that coral fungus, or whatever you call it?"

Whitmore and Brook shared a glance, neither particularly

interested in conversing with the prick. He had lied to them about the threats on this island, gotten two of their group killed, basically gotten them into this mess when they could have simply extracted after the firefight with the strikers. Now, he wanted to act like they were all buddies?

Brook groaned. Despite these facts, he decided to indulge Lee.

"There were some fatal instances in Japan. They didn't eat the stuff, but they brewed tea from it after confusing it with an edible fungus. Brain damage and organ failure was the result of that."

Lee winced at the thought, then casually shrugged.

"So, basically, they consumed the equivalent of my ex-wife's cooking."

Whitmore and Brook glanced at each other again. Gradually, two grins began to take form. Asshole or not, the guy managed to pull off a decent joke.

"That bad, huh?" Whitmore said.

Lee chuckled. "She hosted Thanksgiving one year I was stateside. For a while, I thought it was a blessing. My in-laws got so sick, they never came to visit again." He cocked a smile while shaving off layers of a hoof fungus. "That, and everyone else got food poisoning . . . everyone except me and Lydia."

"The ex?" Whitmore asked.

"No. Her sister." Lee clicked his tongue.

Whitmore clenched his jaw, putting two and two together. "You banged your sister-in-law?"

"What can I say?" Lee said. "Three years of spending my money, poisoning me at the dining room table, and gaining a hundred pounds . . . I needed *something* good out of that marriage."

Whitmore snorted. "You really are a son of a bitch. No wonder the agency hired you."

With that said, the three men allowed themselves a good laugh.

The levity was cut short by the flash of a hot flare. All units turned northwest. Zed was immediately awake and on his feet, weapon in hand.

"Trent? Zed? You guys have any visual?" Whitmore said.

"Not yet," Trent said.

Whitmore looked at the trees where the flare had gone off. There was no movement as far as he could see. The flare had come from the ground. He moved forward with caution, his eyes shifting back and forth to monitor his surroundings.

"Brook, keep your eyes on the trees. We know how our guest likes to set up an ambush."

"You sure you want to go out there?" Lee said.

"If I can get a shot . . ." Whitmore tilted his rifle, putting the grenade launcher on display. He paused, hearing approaching footsteps. They did not appear to be coming from a large six-legged organism, but something bipedal and roughly his size. It wasn't hard to figure out what kind of life form that was.

He backed up, not wanting to get rushed by a horde of drones. Yet, this did not sound like the movements of a large group. Just one human, who might or might not be under the specimen's control. Then again, if the creature wanted to use its drones to flush his team out, why send just one?

Black combat gear emerged from behind the shrubs. Whitmore took aim, only to immediately lower his muzzle after identifying the visitor.

"Delta?"

The mercenary had no weapon and moved somewhat sluggishly, keeping his chin down. His arms were tucked over his stomach, giving the impression that he was sick or wounded.

Deep down, Whitmore was cursing. Had this been anyone else, he and his team would not bother taking a chance. If the person had not identified himself or herself, they would have wasted them on the first sighting. But this was Delta, one of their own.

He continued moving forward, putting his teammates on edge.

"Get away from him," Lee said.

"Wait, wait," Zed said, seeing the way Lee had his rifle positioned. The agent was ready and willing to plant a headshot and eliminate all risk. "He's alone. The thing would not send him out here all alone . . ."

As much as Whitmore didn't like it, he was leaning toward Lee's side of things. He decided he would give Delta one more chance, then take him out at the knees. One thing was different: Delta had closed within sufficient range to sprint at them, yet he continued at this slow pace.

"Delta?! Say something!" For a second, it looked as though the merc was going to comply.

His head tilted up, revealing bloodshot, pupil-less eyes. The arms untucked from his stomach, the levers springing from two hand grenades.

The chemically possessed Delta sprinted, arms outstretched, right into the middle of the group.

All five men whipped around to retreat.

BOOM!!!

Two simultaneous blasts sent Whitmore tumbling head-over-heels. He settled on his back, ears ringing, head pounding. Behind that ringing was distorted sounds. Words, none of which he could make out. As the moments went on, his senses gradually returned. He recognized the tone of those voices. Frantic. Frenzied. Conveying pain.

He sat up and looked over his left shoulder. Zed was face-down on the ground with Brook kneeling over him. He was wavering back and forth, having also been rocked by the blast. In his hands were pliers and sutures.

"Sit still . . . *Lie* still. You've got some shrapnel in your back. It will continue to split you wide open unless I get it out now."

Several yards south of them were Trent and Lee, the latter bleeding from a gash in his forehead. Like Whitmore, he was just now pulling himself together. Trent seemed fine for the most part, aside from being juddered by the concussion.

Whitmore looked up, seeing another flare taking flight. This one came from a tree . . . behind Brook. The lower branches shook, a heavy thud reverberating through the ground.

Whitmore grabbed for his rifle. "Brook! On your six!"

The tracker never had a chance. His body spasmed from a large penetrating object piercing his back. His arms flung to the sides, the medical tools hitting the dirt. His head arched back, his chest puffing out, breastbone bursting through his vest. Following it was the pointed tip of the creature's tail.

Bleeding from his mouth, Brook could do nothing but stare in astonishment at the eighteen inches of segmented tail that stuck out of his body. It raised him off the ground and bent, facing him toward the rest of the creature.

It was in plain sight, savoring the view of its victim skewered on its tail. With eight red eyes, it stared Brook in the face. Multiple mandibles, like spider legs, frolicked over a main jaw that shockingly appeared reptilian in its base shape. The lower jaw was partly open, its white triangular teeth on display. Two large pincers were poised in front of its black body, which, aside from having six legs instead of eight, greatly resembled that of a scorpion.

Those pincers grabbed ahold of Brook, cutting deep and pulling in separate directions. There was a fountain of blood and guts as Brook's body split vertically. The specimen, bathed in scarlet, tossed the limp pieces away and set its sights on its next target.

Zed had rolled onto his side, shouting as he fumbled for his sidearm. The creature darted in his direction, flattening him on his back as it mounted him. The two pincers clamped over his shoulders, pinning him to the dirt.

The stinger struck through his right eye, its mass splitting his skull wide open. Immediately retracting its tail, it turned toward Whitmore.

He was on one knee, finger on the grenade launcher's trigger. Its size did not hinder its speed, demonstrated by its ability to dart into the jungle right as Whitmore fired. The grenade soared over Zed's body where the target had been, exploding several yards in the distance.

He took aim in the direction the creature had run and fired a few bursts.

"Sir?!" Trent said. He was moving toward Whitmore, limping on his left leg. Apparently, he hadn't escaped the grenade blasts unscathed, for a piece of shrapnel protruded from his hamstring.

"We're gonna have to move," Whitmore said. "You all right? Can you run?"

"Not like I have much choice, right, boss?" Trent responded.

The swaying of a branch drew their eyes to the nearest tree. Perched high up was a black insectoid shape, legs digging into the bark, the tail coiling behind its body.

Whitmore pushed Trent to the east. "Go."

The three men retreated into the jungle. Low on supplies and ammo, their last hope for survival rested on making a fast escape. Anything else was a losing battle.

The very reason the U.S. government wanted this thing for themselves.

. . .

IT MOVED DOWN the length of the branch, monitoring the trajectory of its prey. They were heading for the ponds—unknowingly setting themselves up for the perfect trap.

A new chemical signal dispersed from pores in its exoskeleton. It descended from the tree and commenced the chase, making sure to keep the humans running east.

15

"We need to turn left," Lee said. "We're heading straight for the ponds and mud pits."

Whitmore slowed to a stop and looked around to assess the situation. To the left was a valley full of thick jungle. A perfect place for the creature to stalk them. He looked to the right. Everything south was a marshland, a swampy soup mixture of mud, standing water, soggy grass and algae, and vines. After just a few moments of observing, he spotted the bony remains of something that had gotten itself trapped. A boar, by the looks of it.

He looked behind them. No sign of the creature. But Whitmore wasn't fooled. Just because it wasn't in plain sight didn't mean it wasn't there.

Staring straight ahead, he could see the wetness where the marsh hooked to the left, right into their path. The water appeared to be shallow, sparking the hope that maybe they could just wade through it. Whitmore moved close to its edge, tempted to put that theory to the test. Sure enough, going straight was a guaranteed death trap.

Under that layer of water was thick mud that would cling to his boots like glue. Farther out, the water was deeper. Almost waist high. Even if they didn't get stuck in the mud, it would slow them down enough for the bug to close the distance.

Whitmore clenched his teeth, preventing himself from cursing. Now was not the time to lose his head. They were in a tough spot, and for all he knew, this was part of the creature's plan. They couldn't turn back, they couldn't go south or forward, and the only way out of here was a death trap.

"Just a moment," Whitmore said. "Something's not right."

"Damn straight something's not right," Lee said. "We just got our asses kicked. There's no choice. I gotta get someone to bomb this island."

"And how the hell are you gonna do that?" Trent said. "Last I heard, your superiors were a little hesitant, to say the least, about a full-scale aerial assault so close to Chinese territorial waters."

"Simple," Lee said, reaching for his SAT phone. "I'll get a message to the admiral in charge of the Red Lightning. I still have a few codes from my undercover days. That son of a bitch will have no issue with frying this island."

"Assuming he won't just send more men," Whitmore said.

"He's a prick, but he wouldn't do that unless he believed things were under control," Lee said. "Fortunately, I know who the lieutenant was, and I was pretty crafty when hacking his computer. I'll pretend to be him, and—"

Lee froze, watching the water rippling behind Whitmore and Trent. The two men turned around and saw it, immediately stepping away. They could not see anything in the water so far, but they sensed a sinister presence.

"Shit," Lee muttered. He turned to retreat into the jungle. "Come on. This way." He tucked his phone away. The message could wait until later. Right now, he needed to get away from this marsh and whatever was waiting inside it.

He pierced the thick jungle, only to stop after three steps. Not by choice.

Hearing the agent gasping, Whitmore and Trent hurried over to him. Both stood in stunned silence, seeing Lee strung up against a wall of stringy white silk. A giant spiderweb. Only it was no spider that had constructed this death trap.

Secured several feet high in this wall of silk were six large cocoons. Their web casings were wet, freshly woven, the creatures inside shifting about.

"Jesus," Trent muttered. "It's cocooning its victims now?"

Whitmore shook his head. "I don't think those are victims." He took another look at the water, catching a glance of a ripple at the edge of the pond.

He drew a knife and began cutting Lee from the web. Trent assisted, the serrated edge of his blade struggling against the tough silk.

"Hang on, this might work better." Whitmore pulled a lighter from his pocket, sparked a flame, and held it to the web. Like a torch against paper, it cut through effortlessly.

He freed Lee's arms, upper body, and his rifle. As the merc worked on freeing his legs, the agent took aim at one of the cocoons.

Trent stepped back. "What are you doing?"

Lee sawed the cocoon open with a spray of bullets. Its underside peeled apart, dropping its now-dead contents onto the web. The men beheld the sight of a coiled larva, its pink body showing the early signs of developing spines and legs. It was in the beginning stages of metamorphosis.

"Kill them all," Lee said. He immediately shot the next one. The cocoon thrashed, the larva inside awakened by sudden pain before entering a permanent slumber. Trent took the next one, wincing as fluid spilled from the bullet holes. He wasn't generally squeamish, but these things were beyond disgusting, both in their appearance and their life cycle.

They worked their way down, successfully killing the six offspring. Lee was now mostly free from the web, his obsession with killing the creatures forcing Whitmore to step back. He returned with the lighter in hand, burning away at the silk on one leg. He was just about done.

Trent ejected his empty mag. "Whew! I think I've had enough surprises from this place to last me a lifetime."

His statement was punctuated by a splattering noise and a gasp as he was suddenly pulled to the ground.

Whitmore turned around, seeing Trent sliding back, a long line of silk extending from his shoulders. His eyes followed the line to the pond, where another larva had risen. Having taken sanctuary in the shallow water, it was ready to feed. Its little legs, stronger than they appeared, pulled Trent toward the edge of the water.

Whitmore pocketed his lighter and shouldered his rifle. A three-round burst splattered the worm's head and everything within. Trent scampered away from the water's edge and rose to his knees. He faced the water, seeing two more worms rise in hopes of grabbing a bite.

He took the one on the left, taking pleasure in watching its body convulse as it absorbed the lead. Whitmore gunned down the other. The worms fell, their bodies twisting and splashing in the agonies of death.

Trent lowered his weapon and exhaled. "As I was saying—"

A blur of white streaked past Whitmore and splattered on Trent's chest. Once again, he was yanked to the ground. Whitmore turned with his weapon raised, expecting to see another larva in his iron sights.

It was not a pinkish-white spindly worm, but a large, six-legged aberration. The specimen leaned back on its hind legs, having jettisoned a line of silk from its underbelly. Its two pincers pulled the squirming Trent closer, stopping as the beast recognized the aggressive stance of the other human.

It faced Whitmore and fired another line of web. The tip opened like an umbrella, encompassing the barrel of his rifle. In the blink of an eye, the gun was yanked from his grasp.

"Goddammit, Whitmore! Get me out of here!" the panicking Lee shouted.

Whitmore kept his eyes on the arachnoid, drawing his Desert Eagle in a last-ditch attempt to save Trent.

He felt wetness on his back, and in that moment, he was looking to the sky. He fell backward, splashing water and mud. Immediately, he felt the tug of a sticky substance pulling against him, dragging him farther into the pond. Whitmore looked back, seeing a fourth worm angled above the water.

The damn things were birthing everywhere, it seemed.

He managed to roll himself to his knees and point the Desert Eagle at its head. The first shot missed. The next four didn't. The thing fell backward, its line slackening.

Whitmore stood up, only to immediately stumble. His feet were sinking into the mud.

"Shit."

It took maximum effort just to raise his boot a few centimeters. A scream from Trent gave him pause. Stuck in the mud, Whitmore could do nothing but watch as the specimen severed Trent's right arm. It looked at the bloody appendage, determining which side it wanted to start eating from. It chose the bloody stump.

Its mandibles took possession of the snack, freeing its pincers to punish the mercenary further. They pierced his stomach and opened him up, exposing everything inside.

Trent shook and coughed, finally stiffening after many agonizing moments.

The creature stood up, watching Whitmore. Slowly, it advanced. It closed to within the water's edge, merely ten feet from its next victim, who was pitifully stuck in the mud.

A sound of struggle made it turn to its left. It gazed upon the ravaged cocoons and the human trapped near them.

Lee tried to cut away at the remaining strands, hyperventilating as the thing moved closer. He had thought, with its attention on Whitmore, he would have just enough time to free himself and run.

"No, no, no . . . get away from me, you fuck!"

He pointed his weapon, but he was too late. The specimen grabbed him, effortlessly pulling him from the web. It forced him onto his stomach, pinning him.

Lee clawed at the ground, desperate to escape. Not just to escape, but to avoid this horrible fate. He looked over his shoulder. The stinger was bending over the creature's head, its tip pointing at his back.

This could not be happening. Lee knew the risks of this kind of work. There was always a chance of injury, capture, and death. But this? This was beyond all that. He had read the studies. He knew of the reports of hosts still showing brain activity. This was something that was supposed to happen to other people. Not *him*!

Death was preferable. He tried to reach for his pistol in hopes of blowing his brains out. Anything was better than the fate the creature was promising him.

His hand felt his thigh, finding one of its front legs blocking his handgun. Whether deliberately or by happenstance, it would not allow him to foil its plans.

"WHITMORE!!! KILL IT!!!"

Nerves fired throughout his body as the stinger pierced his back. The venom took hold, freezing the agent on the ground. The tiny embryo was now in its new home.

Little by little, Whitmore worked himself free. Lee was neutralized, worse than dead. The specimen turned around, ready to inflict the same fate onto Whitmore.

He successfully freed the other foot, putting himself closer to drier ground.

The beast reared its pincers back, ready to grab him by his shoulders. Escape was not an option. He was still standing in the mud, each step putting him a couple inches deep.

Outrunning the thing was no option either, not at this stage. All there was for him to do was make a last stand or blow his brains out.

Not one to opt out of a fight, Whitmore chose a middle ground. He grabbed two grenades and pulled the pins, holding them out toward the specimen. Only his fingertips kept the levers in place.

"Go ahead. Sting me."

To his surprise, the creature stopped. Twitching its mandibles, it watched him. After a few moments that felt like hours, the creature slowly backed off.

Whitmore inched his way out of the mud, keeping the grenades in plain sight. This thing truly was intelligent. It recognized these explosives. Now, it made sense why Delta had suicided.

Finally on dry land, he stepped toward the jungle. The creature held its ground, knowing an attack would only lead to its own death.

He had to make a decision. This stand-off could not last forever. Staying here was suicide. His only hope was to run. Keeping his eyes on the specimen, he backed into the jungle, making sure to avoid the nest.

The creature remained in place, making no attempt to go after him. Whitmore knew this wouldn't last. No way this thing would give up so easily, if at all. Still, he needed to take advantage of this opportunity. He turned on his heels and sprinted into the jungle.

16

He was alone.

Gerry, Delta, Brook, Trent, Zed, and Lee were dead. Or worse.

Whitmore pressed deeper into the jungle, peeking over his shoulder every few moments. He couldn't see the thing, which in a way was oddly worse than having it on his tail. He stopped long enough to get the pins back into the grenades. With all the obstacles and hazards out here, an explosive accident was bound to happen. During his pause, he made a quick inventory of his supplies.

It was quick indeed. He had the two grenades, the Desert Eagle with two extra mags, his combat knife, one leftover magazine for his M16A2, and one fragmentation round.

He heard the shifting of branches above him. Looking up, he caught a glimpse of the black multi-legged creature passing through the canopy. For all he knew, it was getting in position to lasso him with its projectile web. Back on the hill, it had been unable to get close enough undetected. But now, it had no such worry. There were no other soldiers to back its prey up, no cleverly hidden devices to give away its position.

Whitmore ran, pistol pointed high. A string of web shot from one of the trees, missing him by a yard. His theory proved to be correct. It wanted to seize him from high above, maybe bash him against the trees to stun him and prevent use of the grenades, then sting him.

He fired a shot where the web came from, then resumed his retreat. A hiss reverberated through the jungle, taunting the soldier-for-hire. Whitmore did not look back this time. A mixture of sweat, pond water, mud, and flakes of vegetation covered his body, weighing him down.

A large glob of mud had caked on the underside of his right boot. Twice already, it had nearly caused him to slip and fall. Whitmore was able to maintain his footing—until his boot touched down on another mud puddle hidden behind some thick plants. His foot slipped out from under him as though he had stepped on a sheet of ice.

"Fuck!"

Next thing he knew, he was on his back. Worse—on his back and sliding down a steep wet hill. Wind assaulted his eyes. Plants slapped his face and body. Small animals scattered from the path of the human projectile speeding down the hill.

He arrived at the foot of the hill, the momentum catapulting him forward like a ping pong ball. Whitmore ended up face-down, his mind in a tailspin, his senses in a haze. A deep breath relaxed his mind and body for a precious few seconds, all he needed for his wits to start returning.

The first sense to return was that of smell. That long breath turned into a series of sniffs. There was a repugnant odor in the air. Next came his hearing, which detected a soundtrack of groans, moans, snarls, and motion.

Whitmore's vision cleared, allowing him to see his new surroundings and the details therein. It was more of the same for the most part. A seemingly endless valley of trees and undergrowth—with a horde of chemically-possessed ghouls stumbling toward him.

Walking bodies, in various stages of breakdown, containing the horrified minds of their previous selves, growled as their pupil-less eyes spotted the fresh meat. Whitmore sprang to his feet. He could not tell how many there were, but it was enough to make him nervous.

"My lucky-fucking-day."

The Desert Eagle went to good use, plastering the nearby plants with the brains of the nearest snarling drones. With the bug somewhere behind him, Whitmore knew holding his ground was suicide. He needed to keep running. AND fight along the way.

Directly ahead was a tight group of ghouls. It was more than his Desert Eagle could handle in the few seconds he had. It was a job for one of his grenades.

Whitmore pulled the pin, let the lever spring free, then threw the explosive into the center of the group. An eruption of pure force and shrapnel cut through the five ghouls, rupturing brains and body organs.

Whitmore took off, gunning off another hostile. They were scattered, but all moving in his direction. His running motion along with theirs made headshots extremely difficult. Whitmore had to wait for the targets to get fairly close before shooting at them. The next shot found the forehead of his target, blowing the back of its head out. There were a few misses after that one. Bullets soared through the jungle, some of them missing entirely, others striking a ghoul in the shoulder or chest. The bodily damage did nothing to deter the fiends.

One of them closed within four feet. Whitmore put the gun to its forehead. That shot didn't miss. Seeing the slide locked back, Whitmore ejected the empty mag and slammed a fresh one home. Everywhere he looked, there were drones coming at him. Some far back in the jungle, others inside ten feet.

Whitmore gunned another one down and dashed northeast. At least, he was pretty sure it was northeast. He couldn't get a good look at the sun through the trees. The shadows all blended together; he didn't have an opportunity to check for moss growth on the tree trunks, nor did he have time to get a good look at the sun's position, for his attention was monopolized by the enemy.

He shot another, then another, and another. More still came, holding no regard for the dangers this prey carried. Bullets punched through flesh and flora, their accuracy and effectiveness hampered by fatigue and constant motion.

Having wasted two shots on a target approaching from the east, Whitmore forced himself to stop and take a proper shooting stance. The ghoul's head split apart, the knees buckling under the dead weight. Panting, Whitmore pivoted to the right, just in time to foil another ghoul's attempt to bite him. Its jaws snapped shut, not on flesh, but cold steel. Its next taste was of hot lead, a sensation which did not last even a tenth of a second.

In that moment, Whitmore felt bony fingers close over his shoulders. The ghoul behind him pulled Whitmore backward with surprisingly powerful force near equivalent to that of a powerlifter. Teeth closed over his trapezius. Only the tough material of his vest prevented the teeth from immediately cutting into him.

Whitmore turned and pushed against the ground with all his might, propelling himself and his attacker backwards against the trunk of a tree. The impact shook the ghoul, loosening its grip enough for Whitmore to pull away. He spun to face the man-thing, cratering its skull with a point-blank shot.

It was a situation that brought new meaning to the phrase 'no rest for the weary.' More drones were still coming at him. If there was any bright side to the situation, it was that Whitmore could actually count them. There were twelve now, coming from different directions.

Down to one mag, there were more hostiles than he had bullets. The one thing in his favor was that four of them were in a tight group. It was a job for his second grenade.

Out came the pin. Whitmore tossed the explosive in their path. BOOM! Their bodies came apart, spilling their insides onto the ground. The others showed no concern for their dead brethren. Even now, they were single-minded in their pursuit of prey.

Whitmore slammed the last magazine into place. It took two shots to take down the next target. Two more for the next one. Whitmore was getting frustrated. There was once a time when he would NEVER miss a shot, regardless of his physical state. Then again, his younger self would probably never have survived this long against ravenous zombies, web-spitting worms, and a prehistoric scorpion-bug-thing.

There were six of them left.

BANG!

At least that shot was up to standard. Five to go.

Actually, SIX, counting the damn larva that followed him from the marshy area. Had he not been so preoccupied, he likely would have detected the creature earlier. For the second time, Whitmore was yanked to the ground by a sticky stream of web.

He growled, feeling his body being dragged toward the creature's mandibles. He shifted his body, positioning himself on his knees. The larva was positioned like a cobra, casually tugging on the string like a fisherman would reel in his line.

Three of his four remaining bullets put this last offspring out of his misery. Standing up, he turned around to fire his last shot at one of the advancing ghouls. Fortunately, this final bullet was well placed. UNFORTUNATELY, he was out of ammo, and still had four ghouls to go.

Whitmore slowed his breathing and remained still for the next couple of moments. It was the closest thing to a rest he was going to get. He pulled his knife from its sheath and shifted his weight, poising himself for the inevitable clash.

Boots kicked up dirt and grass as he charged at the ghouls. Tucking his head down, he rammed one of them head-on, knocking it to the ground. Down came the knife, straight through its eye socket into its brain.

Whitmore stood up and slashed at the next one. The blade passed through its cheeks, widening its jaw like a snake's. It also allowed better access to the roof of the mouth, where Whitmore's blade plunged. Its tip exited out the back of the skull, destroying the precious organ inside.

The only problem with this tactic was the struggle to free his knife. It was lodged in there pretty good, leaving him no choice but to abandon it, as the last two were nearly on top of him.

Whitmore backed away, watching those teeth dripping toxic saliva. The two ghouls kept pace, their arms outstretched like Hollywood movie monsters. Fed up with retreating, Whitmore threw a kick, striking one square in the chest. As it fell over, the second one closed the distance, grabbing Whitmore by the vest and pulling itself in for a bite.

Whitmore spun, toppling himself and the drone over a fallen branch. He put himself on top of the thing, pried the MP-443 Grach from the holster on its hip, and put the muzzle to its forehead.

BANG!

No sooner did the brains paint the ground than Whitmore felt the grip of the last drone close over his vest. He was yanked backward and slammed against the root of the tree. He felt the pistol bounce from his grip, leaving him defenseless yet again.

Defenseless. There was no such thing. Not for Whitmore.

He rose a foot and pushed the drone off him before it could bite. Springing up, he ran at the ghoul, tackling it to the ground. Mounted atop it, he pounded its face with rock-hard fists. Bare knuckles plowed the nose and eye sockets, carefully avoiding the teeth and the toxins they carried.

Spitting and seething, Whitmore continued the bombardment. Its head bounced against the ground with each hit, rocking the brain.

The arms fell to the side, the jaw went slack, the snarling ceasing. The ghoul was dead, the poor soul inside liberated.

Whitmore was back on his feet, feeling as though his heart would burst at any moment. He took in the silence, relieved, and amazed that he had come through this ordeal alive.

The only one more surprised was the bug.

Whitmore looked up and to the left, seeing it descend from the tree. Like a massive six-legged feline, it landed on the ground, its eyes on the dead hosts. The larvae inside were too weak to survive without pre-digested sustenance.

It turned toward Whitmore.

The mercenary held his ground, more irritated than alarmed by this point.

"I swear, if I make it out of this mess alive, I'll be opening up a pesticide and exterminator business."

He took a step back once the creature started coming his way. On the fourth step, he nearly tripped over one of the bodies. His eyes went down long enough for him to find his footing. In doing so, he got a glimpse of the dead striker's vest, and the two gas canisters in the left pouches. His mind flashed to the southeast part of the island, where they had found the dead boars and mass insect and bird fatalities resulting from the Red Lightning's attempt to kill the creature. They may not have been successful, but that didn't mean the gas was not effective.

Only one way to find out.

Whitmore pulled the canisters from the striker, pulled the pins, and tossed them between himself and the specimen. The creature reared back and hissed, swiping its pincers at the toxic fumes spewing from those gray canisters.

Whitmore took the opportunity and ran.

Fatigue ate at his muscles right away, driving home the fact he would have to hide or somehow make a last stand. The latter was impossible at this time. If only he'd had the chance to salvage a few guns from those bodies back there. Alas, hiding was the only course of action.

He found a tree rising from the side of an oddly shaped hill. Its roots were rather exposed, forming a little spiderweb of wood under its base.

It was as good a place as any. Whitmore slipped inside, squeezing between two of the roots. As he settled in, he learned he had not been the only one who ever considered this to be a good place of shelter. The ground had been dug out at some point, possibly by a boar. This abandoned den served as a blessing for Whitmore, as it allowed him to fit his entire body under this tree.

It was a good shelter. A good hiding place? Against most enemies, maybe. Against the bug? Not so much.

"Shit."

He saw the creature enter the area. It only took a few moments of searching before it zeroed in on the roots.

Whitmore tucked himself back as best he could. The pincers opened, splintering the root barrier between the creature and the human. The tail was in position, dripping venom from its tip.

Cursing, Whitmore tried to back away even farther. There was nowhere else to go. He was trapped under this massive plant, his body rubbing against something rough and dry.

Tinder fungus.

Whitmore gave the hoof-shaped growths an admiring glance. An idea came to mind. Desperate times called for desperate measures, after all. He dug a pocketknife from his pants and unfolded it. The combat knife would have worked better, but beggars couldn't be choosers. He slid the blade against the fungus, making several thin shavings. He mixed them with some dry grass that made for bedding in the den, courtesy of the boar that previously resided here.

Next, he removed the bullet casings from a couple M16A2 rounds, striking their gunpowder over the little pile of tinder. He opened three more bullet casings, keeping them upright like a set of shot glasses.

With the shavings on a twelve-inch piece of bark, dressed in gunpowder, it was time to put this makeshift plan to work. The bug finally severed the thick roots between it and its prey, tiny shavings clinging to the serrated edges. It peered at the fresh meat inside, and the strange bark plate full of tinder in front of him.

"Let me add some kick to your snack."

He lit the lighter and put the flame to the shavings. The gunpowder particles lit up instantly, the grass and fungus catching hold of that flame.

The creature hesitated, caught off guard by the sight and heat of fire. Even more surprising was the sudden flinging of that fire onto its face. The heat tripled as Whitmore took the three casings full of gunpowder and, like splashing someone in a bar with a drink, flung the flammable particles onto the flame.

The bug scurried backward, its face and neck ablaze. Its interest in capturing Whitmore had vanished in favor of putting an end to this agonizing torture. Brushing its claws over its face, it tried to scrape the fire off. When that didn't work, it resorted to darting far into the jungle.

Whitmore, after several moments of stunned silence, could not help but chuckle. Years of training, access to the most advanced weaponry and technology, and it was fire—the most primitive invention of all—that fended off the specimen.

He wasn't complaining.

17

Never in his life had Whitmore appreciated the warmth and crackling sounds of a simple fire as much as he did now. After the creature left, he remained hunkered down, unsure if it would return in the next minute or so. If it did and he had exited this little safe haven, it would have little trouble getting the jump on him. So far, there was no sign of it. Sure enough, even the most ferocious of beasts disappeared when pure hot fire came into the equation. Especially if their eyes were singed.

Whitmore fed the flames that accumulated outside the tree root barrier, using them as a deterrent in case the thing came back. There was no motion in the trees. No sound. Nothing. That did not necessarily mean it was gone. The only way to know for sure was to step out and see if he would get attacked.

After about ten minutes of rest, Whitmore emerged into the open. He held his arms out, daring the specimen to attack.

Nothing.

It was gone, the damage to its face significant enough to keep it away. At least, for now.

Sooner or later, it would be back. By now, Whitmore had a good read on the thing. It was an intelligent creature that also carried a grudge. No way would it let him off scot-free after killing its young and burning its face.

Perhaps he could make it to the shore. The bug had retreated west, and he needed to go east. The odds were much more favorable than they were twenty minutes ago.

Two things kept Whitmore from leaving. For one, that thing could be anywhere. For all he knew, it would be waiting to intercept him at the beach or somewhere along the way.

Secondly, Whitmore had lost all interest in running away from this fight. He was too pissed off.

Observing the surrounding wilderness, Whitmore's mind went to work planning his revenge. Sooner or later, the creature would be back. And when it did, he would be ready. Though he had no weapons, that did not mean he was truly unarmed. All around him were resources that were more than sufficient in bringing down the bug.

Just a few yards into the jungle was a large broken branch, laying in a heap of dried grass. There was more tinder fungus to be harvested. The trees were covered in thick vines. So many things to be used as spears, trip wires, dead weights, even as shovels and cooking dishes.

Prepping all these natural tools would be much easier with his combat knife.

With that in mind, Whitmore initiated the first part of his plan, to return to the valley where he fought the ghouls.

It was a sight he was all too used to by now. So many bodies, men who could have been so much more had their circumstances been different. The insects on the island hadn't wasted any time helping themselves to some of the strikers. Whitmore secured a couple pistols and several spare magazines. By themselves, the weapons were insufficient to fight the thing, but it was a start.

He entered a misty area where the gas canisters had

dispersed. On the ground was the knife, still lodged in the striker's skull. He pried it loose, then looked at the dead man's vest. There were a couple gas grenades in his pouch, holding a chemical agent inside that metal casing that the specimen clearly did not like.

Whitmore seized the grenades, then checked a few other bodies, securing several more. In addition to gas grenades, he secured several fragmentation grenades.

With these deadly tools at his disposal, Whitmore was ready to begin forging his defensive position.

18

In the hours that passed, Whitmore worked relentlessly. The first course of action was chopping down vines and thinning some of them out. Next, he found himself climbing several trees like Tarzan, though with a more modern and deadly motive.

He made various uses of the dead branches, ranging from simple punji sticks to shaping a makeshift shovel, which went to good use. During his prep, he periodically used some of the gas grenades, assuring himself that the bug was not attempting to sneak up on him.

Once the punji sticks were in place, it came time to put that shovel to use. A muddy area on the east side of this hideout served as the location for this special trap. Sweat ran down Whitmore's body in large, dirty beads. He did not slow, for time was of the essence.

When the trap was dug, it was time to blanket it with a makeshift net covered in leaves and grass . . . as well as bark and tinder fungus. When Whitmore completed that task, it came time for his cooking skills to come into play.

In scouting the area for resources, he came across his special ingredient. First, he needed a pot. He may not have had cookware handy, but he did have a log. Laying it on one side, he plunged his knife repeatedly into the top, chipping out the insides until he had a large wooden bowl.

Next, he made a campfire. His lighter proved useful in speeding up this process. Using his knife, he held the special ingredient over the flames, drying it out. With his smaller pocketknife, he cut it into tiny shavings. As he did that, his wood bowl was held over the fire by a few used canisters. The fire itself was in a hole, giving more space between the embers and the bowl. Inside the bowl was water from his canteen and some jungle vines, gradually coming to a boil thanks to the flame underneath.

The herbs went in, brewing into a special mixture. While this went on, Whitmore dug out more of this special ingredient, making sure not to touch it with his bare skin. Using a casing made of wet leaves, he squeezed the thing until it was a slimy mush.

All the while, he reflected on his life.

It seemed there were two separate lifetimes he had lived. The one he thought of most was the one he was in currently. It started two months after his eighteenth birthday. That first day of basic training, he was the only recruit who relished the so-called abuse from the military staff. Every time a drill sergeant got in his face, he felt energized. That was when he first knew he was made for this life. All the conflicts since were nothing more than tasks on a whiteboard to be completed. Completed *well*, to be specific. There were a few purple hearts along the way and medals for valor. He shrugged those things off. The greatest award was fighting an enemy and being the one left standing.

The other lifetime comprised the eighteen years and two months prior to that fateful day. Whitmore had not come from a military family. His grandfather had served in World War II on the western front, but other than that, he was the only one in his family tree to serve. As a kid, he partook in regular sports such as football and hockey, received a black belt in Shotokan karate, and helped out his father with his home repair business.

For the first time in what felt like forever, Whitmore thought of that first life. He always tried to force the memories back. They weren't compatible with his current self. Those were the days before a life of killing. Whitmore never took a life that was not actively trying to take his or that of some innocent person, but it was a hard existence all the same. To live it, he could not dwell on the tranquil days of his youth.

Now, he was faced with the reality of his current existence. It was one of nonstop war and death. Yet, no victory. Yes, battles were frequently won. That was why Whitmore was considered the best. However, it was one fight after another, with no end in sight. Except for the dead.

What was the point in fighting if there was no end? Sure, Whitmore considered himself to be a warrior, and many warriors considered death on the battlefield to be the honorable way to go. But as he saw on this island, this wasn't simply a battle of good versus evil, but rather factions hiding in the dark, manipulating things and stirring conflict.

Whitmore told himself he was okay with that. As long as the money was right. But seeing his men slaughtered like cattle forced him to stare into the cold reality of this life. There were only two ends. One was death and whatever afterlife that followed. The other was to embrace a new life. That, or the old one.

With that thought came the intrusive memory of spearfishing on the river with his father.

"*Balance.*"

He planted his feet on the ground. His eyes were on the river. Just a few inches underneath was a fifteen-inch carp.

"*Form your T-stance.*"

He shifted his left leg toward the bug, using his throwing arm to keep himself steady.

"Breathe. Breathe." His father's voice was calm and slow. *"Do not take your eyes off of the fish. Balance and breathe. Let everything disappear except you and your target. Focus . . ."*

Other memories included going on worksites with his old man. He owned a home repair business, which he'd started in his early twenties. At seventy-three, the man was still going at it. Whitmore always told himself his father enjoyed working, plain and simple. He was the best at his craft and was in high demand, just like his son. What man wouldn't take advantage of that?

Only now did Whitmore acknowledge the truth. Though his old man did prefer to stay active, it was not the sole reason he worked in his later years. It was not easy living a life waiting for that terrible phone call saying your son was killed in action. His father never lectured him on his career choices. Even as a retired sergeant major starting his own paramilitary unit, Whitmore only got two phrases from his dad.

"I love you, son."

"You're always welcome home."

Images of his team flashed in his mind. Gerry, Delta, Brook, Zed, and Trent. Each one had provided Whitmore with a special contact in case the worst ever was to happen. Trent had a wife in Wisconsin whom he sent his earnings to. He didn't talk about her much, only because those good aspects of his life were kept for himself, not to be shared.

Zed had a brother somewhere in Texas. Whenever he was free, he made sure to visit. Those were the few times Zed lived anything even remotely resembling a normal life.

Gerry had a sister in Seattle. She was recently divorced, her time mostly spent waitressing while attending college. His finances would be transferred to her account in the event of his death, something which regrettably had come true.

Delta had no family that Whitmore was aware of. His parents had both passed away years prior, the father from cancer, the mother from a heart attack not long after. He was the only child, with no aunts, uncles, or cousins. His family was his team. Aside from them, he had an old Army buddy in Ohio whom he had stayed in touch with over the years.

Brook had folks in Montana. They were ranchers working on two thousand acres of land. Of all the calls he would have to make, that was the one Whitmore was dreading the most.

That brought his mind full circle back to his own father. For decades, all he'd wanted was for his boy to return home. He had done enough fighting as far as his dad was concerned.

Whitmore knew one thing: should the bug triumph over him, there would be two deaths, not just one. One way or another, his father would get the news. The toll would be too great. On top of that, the man would have no more purpose in life. The endless work was mainly a way of passing the time and being productive while waiting for his son to return.

Whitmore had already lost his new family. No way would he let that bastard of a bug rob him of his old one too. Nor would it rob the lives of any others. God had cast that beast into extinction for a reason.

It was time to set things right.

19

It was sometime in the evening when Whitmore heard the WHOOSH of one of his traps. It came from the southwest, barely beyond his field of view.

With a pistol in each hand, Whitmore rose from his campfire. So far, there was no movement in the trees that he could see, but that didn't mean the thing wasn't up there.

A growling sound came from the direction of the trap. The creature was not there, but instead had sent one of its drones. The sergeant major moved in, ready to start blasting away at the horde that may or may not have been with the drone.

He was relieved to see there was only one, and that his snare trap had worked. The vines were as flexible as rope, the noose tightening around the intruder's foot. It dangled upside down from the branch of a tree, arms waving chaotically. Toxic saliva dripped from its mouth.

Whitmore stopped, recognizing the boots and gear. This was not a striker . . .

He pushed its shoulder, turning it around to face him. The thing that was once Agent Lee snarled at him. The arms slashed at him, determined to pull him close. Behind that feral snarl was a screaming mind.

Whitmore sighed. He had not cared much for the agent. Hell, the idiot was partly responsible for all of this. The files to replicate the process were right there in his vest, secured in a thumb drive.

If anyone deserved this fate, it was Lee. While that may be true, Whitmore felt a pang of pity spark up. Maybe Whitmore was getting soft. His younger self very well might have left him to suffer this fate. Ultimately, it did not matter what someone deserved or didn't deserve. Allowing this to go on was wrong, plain and simple.

He turned Lee around so he wouldn't have to see it coming.

BANG!

The body went limp, the soul liberated. Where it went from here was not up to Whitmore.

He dug through the vest, finding the thumb drive. Such a small piece of technology, yet it held the secrets for a potential extinction-level event.

A new sound pierced the jungle. Rotor blades.

Whitmore looked to the sky. He couldn't see the helicopter, but there was no doubt in his mind it was on approach for a landing. It sounded to be heading eastward, probably to set down at the dock area.

With its presence came a deadly realization.

Whitmore grabbed the SAT phone from Lee's vest. Sure enough, a code had been sent out.

Christ, the thing used him to bring more people to this island.

SPLAT!

It felt as if a ball of slime had splattered on his chest. The sergeant major was hoisted off the ground, the white substance stretching, the net strands connected to a single rope that led into the trees.

Perched on a branch was the bug. Two pincers pulled its prey closer while its tail coiled into striking position. Its face had a blistery texture that had not been present before. Three of its eyes were gone, covered by this strange resin which seemed to serve as a scab.

Whitmore cursed. He had allowed himself to get duped by the thing. It had sent Lee in as a distraction, knowing it could get into position while his attention was on the agent.

You are getting soft, Sergeant Major.

He drew his knife and put the blade to the web. Very quickly, he learned there was not nearly enough time to cut himself free. The web was attached to his shirt and vest. The only way to go free was to disrobe. Fortunately, it was not on his pants.

He made sure to grab his lighter and pocketknife before cutting through the vest straps and his shirt. He fell free, landing hard on his back.

The haziness brought from impact did not stop the shirtless Whitmore from firing both pistols into the tree. The bug snarled, dropping its worthless catch, and shifting position.

Whitmore stood up and moved east.

"What's the matter? You scared?!"

The bug fired another web strand. This one missed the sergeant major, landing near his feet.

As he suspected, the creature knew he was up to something. Maybe it did not know specifically what his plan was, but it definitely knew this was not a simple matter of going mano-y-mano on a ground-level fight.

Whitmore anticipated this.

Firing a few more shots into the trees, he retreated east. The bug followed, its long body jolting the tree limbs.

After several yards, Whitmore stopped. He backpedaled a few yards while the bug watched him. It was almost directly above him now. Though intelligent and cautious, it saw no threat from the vine he grabbed. It ran up the trunk, all the way to a couple of branches. It was at that point it noticed the human was pulling TWO vines.

Such a useful tool. They could be used for anything, so long as the handler knew what he was doing. They could be used for harnesses, knots, nets, and so much more.

In this case, it was for yanking the pins of grenades that had been fastened to the tree branches.

The creature recognized the sounds of levers detaching. Four grenades, their pins attached two-at-a-time to the vine-ropes, burst with thunderous force. The tree limb folded, attached to the tree by only a few strands. Pieces of bark and vegetation rained down.

In the middle of this storm was the bug. Its arms and legs whipped about as it plummeted to the earth, landing with a heavy thud. Yellow blood oozed from breaches in its belly and left side where the shockwave and shrapnel had hit it directly. It righted itself very quickly and faced Whitmore. It didn't care about stinging him anymore and having the satisfaction of this opponent carrying its offspring. It had a primal urge to rip him open and feast on his guts while he was still alive.

Only the sight of several more vines in Whitmore's hands gave it pause. There were four of them, all running along the ground to their various endpoints.

He yanked them all at once.

A chemical fog filled the air between the bug and him. Whitmore had the ability and discipline to hold his breath. The bug, which breathed through its sides, did not have that luxury.

The flustered creature staggered backward, shrieking as the gas made contact with its exoskeleton. Retreating several yards, its rear leg struck a tripwire made from vines. Hearing movement from the trees on its left, it turned to face the new threat. It was not ready for the sight of a large rock, lined with punji sticks, swinging from a vine straight into its face.

The spiked ball crashed into the target, rupturing one of its scabs. The bug was driven backward. Now even more pissed off, it faced Whitmore and opened its claws with intent to open him up.

He stood directly in front of it. In his hands was a wood bowl with a watery mixture inside.

"I brewed you some tea. Sorry if it's a little bitter."

He thrust the bowl outward. The brew, orange with the shavings of fire coral fungus—his special ingredient—splashed the bug's face. Toxins seeped through its wounds and pores. Like a liquid pesticide, the mixture wreaked havoc on its internal organs and respiratory system. Nerves fired signals to its brain, which was immediately fogging up.

Whitmore stood by, watching the creature suffer. Its pain was obvious, as was its dumbfoundedness.

He moved to the next tree, making sure to be out of the way before triggering the next booby trap. The yank of a vine sent another spiked ball hurtling at the bug. For a second time, it was struck in the face and knocked backward . . . right into the pit Whitmore had dug in the muddy ground. The vine mesh buckled under the creature's weight, dropping it into the shallow trap. It had been the best Whitmore could do in the time he had, but it was enough. Besides, it wasn't about the depth of the pit, but what was in there with the bug.

This is where the lighter came into play. Whitmore lit a torch, the long-dried grass igniting instantly.

Into the pit it went, landing under the bug, right atop the layer of tinder, grass, and gunpowder from his spare bullets. A massive red flame reached high, encompassing the bug. Like the very hand of Satan, it roasted its victim in its grip.

Whitmore stood back and watched as the creature screeched

and thrashed. It had gone mad with pain and infection, having lost all sense of direction. Even the three-foot depth of the pit seemed too steep for it to scale at this point.

Many phrases passed through Whitmore's mind. So many things he would like to say to the dying beast. Ultimately, he settled for silence—aside from the monster's hissing and shrieking.

Behind those screams came the sound of rotor blades. He looked up, catching a glimpse of two helicopters passing overhead. They had been circling the island, possibly in an attempt to make radio contact with the island's Red Lightning unit. With no response, they appeared to be enroute to land, probably near the docks.

He needed to leave now. After all, he did not survive this ordeal just to be killed by a half-assed recovery team.

Into the jungle he went, leaving the specimen to roast in a bath of hell fire.

It let out a deafening hiss. It was a call fueled not by pain, but by anger.

Anger and determination.

20

Streams of sunlight stretched horizontally from the west, the few rays that penetrated the jungle appearing like orange lasers. Whitmore watched his shadow dancing in front of him as he ran east. He could no longer hear the chopper rotors, which meant that the birds had dropped off their units.

He turned to the right, pointing himself southeast. The strike teams—he was certain that's what they were—would likely inspect the dock area first. With some luck, they would be busy in that location long enough for him to get his gear and take off.

Before long, he could see the ocean. The sun's rays were glinting off its surface, giving the beach and this portion of the jungle a warm, welcoming feeling. For Whitmore, only the sea was welcoming. The beach, the jungle, the entire island, as far as he was concerned, could go to hell.

He went from a hard sprint to a dead stop. Those horizontal rays reflected back at him, not from golden sparkles in the water, but from two bluish dots. Eyes. Not human, but beast.

The boar was a full-grown adult, appearing to weigh close to two hundred pounds. It was looking right back at him, shifting its weight forward as though to charge.

Whitmore thought of the two boar carcasses found near the gas grenades. It was not only humans that bug was infecting. The only question: was this boar infected, or just plain pissed off?

Whitmore didn't feel like waiting for an answer. He drew his knife and charged at the thing, snarling like an animal himself.

The boar, *not* infected with the bug's venom, turned north and ran. Whitmore stopped and watched the animal's retreat. Having been sure the damn thing was zombie-fied, he had to laugh.

"I guess I've gotten so accustomed to things going wrong, that a killer zombie boar didn't seem too far out of the ordinary."

A bullet of red flame took to the sky. The boar shrieked, darting from the trip flare it had just set off.

Whitmore's laugh came to an end. "Aw, hell."

Right away, he could hear running feet coming his way. A lot of them. Whitmore saw flashlights beaming into the jungle, then muzzle flashes. The boar squealed and fell on its side. The platoon advanced past it, firing several shots in Whitmore's direction. They missed deliberately, conveying the message that if he made one wrong move, he was a dead man.

The unit leader approached, barking orders to his men in Mandarin. They circled Whitmore, removed his knife, canteen, and pistols, then pushed him to the open beach area. There, they forced him to his knees.

Surrounded by men in black uniforms, Whitmore remained quiet. As he feared, Lee had done the specimen's bidding and alerted the Red Lightning, luring them into a trap. There was at least a dozen of them on this beach, with a few others still in the jungle nearby.

The leader, a captain, stepped in front of Whitmore.

"How many more are you?" he said in English.

"There were seven of us," Whitmore said. "The others are on the mainland with your mother."

Needless to say, the captain did not take kindly to that, as he demonstrated by striking Whitmore in the jaw.

"You are an American, I see." The captain eyed Whitmore, taking notice of his condition. He barked an order at one of his men, who performed another search of Whitmore's pockets. The striker held up the flash drive, taken from Agent Lee's corpse.

The captain took the device and looked at Whitmore. "So, it was you who sabotaged the base."

"It was already a mess," Whitmore said.

"You Navy? Marines?" the captain said. Whitmore didn't answer. One of the men struck him from behind, knocking him face-down into the sand. The captain put a boot on his neck. "Trust me, we WILL get you to talk. You can tell me now, and maybe spare yourself a lot more pain."

Whitmore lifted his head. "All right, you win." The captain lifted his foot and awaited an answer. Whitmore pushed himself up onto his knees, appearing like a man defeated. "You see all this?" He gestured at his shirtless muscular figure. "Your mother wanted to reenact *Naked and Afraid*, so we came out here and—"

He was knocked on his back by a kick to the chest. The captain stood over him, knife in hand.

"Oh, you'll be afraid, all right."

Two strikers grabbed Whitmore by the arms, pinning him. The captain started kneeling, the blade in search of its entry point. A blast of noise from his radio straightened his posture.

Panicked sounds and gunfire echoed from the receiver. The captain spoke into the radio in Mandarin, his tone defining that he was demanding to know what was going on. A frightened striker started to respond, only to scream. The transmission turned to sudden silence.

Whitmore was looking to the northwest. He could hear the rifle shots coming from the jungle. This second striker unit was not too far away. The gunshots soon went silent, leaving the current squad in stunned silence.

The captain ordered his sentries out of the jungle. The squad branched out, now on high alert. The captain repeatedly tried to raise someone from the other team on the radio, but nobody would answer. His attention went back to the sergeant major, who was still held down by his men.

"You have men out there?"

Whitmore barely heard him. His thoughts were focused on what was really out there. He was certain it had been doomed to perish in that fire.

The sentries emerged from the jungle. The captain stared at them, confused. They looked at each other, then at the jungle.

After having a back-and-forth with his men in Mandarin, the captain knelt by Whitmore. "Answer me. Who is out there?!"

By the way he spoke, it was evident the captain was starting to piece together the truth. He had been informed that the situation on this island had been contained. Seeing the sabotage of the base during the aerial recon and then finding this American infiltrator, it was easy to assume an outside entity had been responsible for the recent events. Yet, he realized this mercenary had been fleeing from something before he had been captured. Perhaps . . .

"The specimen? Is it still alive?"

An answer came from the trees. A projectile of white adhesive lashed through the squad, its mesh-like end striking the captain's chest. He was yanked off his feet and pulled toward the trees with spectacular force. All eyes turned to the huge black shape that pulled him into its grasp.

Whitmore felt relieved and cheated all at once. He'd been sure the bug was on the verge of death. Its suffering was illustrated in its appearance. Its shell had faded gray where the fire had scorched it.

More noticeable was its complete lack of caution. No longer did the bug care about stealth and strategy. The toxins in its system had driven it to madness. Only one cognitive function remained.

Murder.

The captain was seized by the two claws. He had enough time to let out a high-pitched squeal before he was ripped in two. Tossing the two halves aside, the bug tore into the squad.

Chaos followed. Military tactics and strategy went right out the window, replaced by sheer panic. The bug grabbed ahold of one of the strikers, raising him over its head and pile-driving him head-first into the ground. The striker's skull popped on contact, the rest of the body shaking from nerves and tremors.

The bug lashed with its tail, decapitating another striker who attempted to pull off a close-range shot. More soldiers fired at it, missing as it darted toward its next victim. That unfortunate individual tried to make a run for it, only to have his legs taken out from under him. Literally. He hit the ground, blood spurting from the stubs where his knees used to be. The bug raced over him, its pincers clinging to the severed limbs.

One of its own legs came down on the helpless soldier, its pointed tip running out his back.

It moved at cheetah speed, the remaining strikers failing to land many shots against its shell. Though heavily damaged from its battle with Whitmore, the exoskeleton was strong enough to withstand the few bullets that made contact.

Whitmore felt the grips on his arms and shoulders loosen, the two soldiers torn between keeping him secured or engaging the bug. The sergeant major made that decision easy. He swung his legs up, kicking one of them in the face. With that soldier knocked to the ground, Whitmore had the leverage to grab the other by the throat. The striker's eye bulged as the iron grip crushed his trachea. Whitmore released his grip, only to pull the man close and knock him out with an elbow to the face.

He grabbed one of the AK-74s and stood up. At his ten o'clock, one of the strikers quickly took notice of him. Whitmore found himself in the middle of a bizarre twist of fate, battling alongside the specimen against these enemy soldiers.

He beat the soldier to the draw, taking him down with a shot to the head. Another saw the man go down and turned to fire a shot at Whitmore. His effort was foiled, not by the mercenary, but by the bug's tail. Its stinger punched through his chest, lifted him off the ground, and flung him into the water.

The beast shuddered, its exoskeleton splintering as several rounds struck its lower back. Pain heightened its rage. In the blink of an eye, it turned around and blasted its web projectile. One of the three strikers was caught by his shoulder and yanked forward. As he stumbled, his body jolted as though struck by lightning. It wasn't electricity tearing through him, but the bullets from his comrades.

They ceased firing and stared in stunned horror, realizing their fellow soldier had been pulled into their line of fire. Their pause proved to be their downfall. The bug closed the distance, slashing one of them across the face with its pincers. It rammed the other, flooring him. Before that striker could even think about righting himself, he was hit in the stomach by the bug's stinger. The tail whipped back, only to sting again. Then again. Then again. It did not bother injecting toxins or embryos. Its purpose was solely to kill as painfully as possible.

While it dealt this punishment, Whitmore made his way to one of the striker captain's halves. Even in war, it wasn't a normal thing to dig through the pockets of half a man, but in this instance, it was a necessary oddity. He found his knife, the thumb drive, and one other item they had taken off him . . . his canteen.

A simple, inconsequential item at first glance, it contained something highly important.

He looked in the bug's direction. It had slaughtered another striker in gruesome fashion and was now attacking the last pair. It took a few hits as it charged them, caring little about the pain and damage, as long as it fulfilled its bloodlust. Its tail went to use, knifing one of them through the neck. The other was grabbed by the pincers and pulled toward the jaws.

Whitmore looked away, gaining no pleasure from seeing the man's legs kicking while his face was mauled. He ran into the jungle as fast as he could. Once the bug was finished with that soldier, he would be next.

21

The soldier took a long time to die, his screams reaching far into the jungle. His prolonged agony, while tragic, worked in Whitmore's favor, granting him time to put several hundred feet of distance between himself and the bug.

He knew the thing would track him down. Even with the fungal toxins coursing through its system, it had managed to follow him for over two miles. The only thing that would bring its wrath to a halt was death.

Whitmore came to a stop. He was close to the area where his team had originally come ashore. Near the base of one of the trees was a flare armed by a tripwire, one of many his men had had to avoid when they arrived.

With minutes at best to plan for what would undoubtedly be his final encounter with the creature, he gave the area a visual inspection for tools to battle it with. He had the AK-74 with half a mag, which was unlikely to finish the thing off, even in its current condition. That was the reason he had made it a point to retrieve his canteen.

He unscrewed the cap, immediately getting a whiff of the mashed-up fungus inside. Direct contact with the bloodstream would cause organ shutdown, brain damage, and respiratory arrest in a human. Considering the bug was already poisoned, it was reasonable to think another dose would finish the job.

"Better fucking work."

He found a low-hanging branch and began hacking away with his knife. Severing the seven-foot limb, he quickly trimmed it, then cut the end into a spear tip.

He was roughly twenty feet from that trip flare. A good hit from a solid object would set it off. Whitmore found a rock, tucked it under his arm, and ascended the tree.

The screams had come to a deathly stop. Silence alerted the sergeant major to the approaching horror. Common sense and experience served as a radar, indicating that it was following his trail.

Whitmore perched himself on a branch several yards in the air. Shielded by the canopy, he watched as the bug came into view. It bled from several wounds, the largest being a nine-inch-wide breach in its lower back. Its tail dragged behind it, the rear legs appearing sluggish in their movements. The pincers, on the other hand, were cocked and ready to lash out.

The beast slowed as it neared the end of the trail. It seemed to be in a state of confusion, not yet grasping the possibility that its prey was stalking it behind the cover of the trees.

Whitmore carefully opened his canteen again and coated the tip of his spear with its contents. His focus went to the wound in the creature's lower back, the only viable place to sink the poison rod.

Twelve feet to its eight o'clock was the trip flare. With the spear ready to go, there was nothing left to do except commit to the plan.

Whitmore threw the rock. It hit the ground and rolled over the wire, triggering the flare. The bug turned to its left, pincers raised, its back exposed to the predator in the tree.

A strong hand gripped the spear. Whitmore raised it over his shoulder, his other hand serving as a crosshair as he steadied his aim.

"Balance."

He planted his feet on two separate branches.

"Form your T-stance."

Whitmore shifted his left leg toward the bug, using his throwing arm to keep himself steady.

"Breathe. Breathe." His father's voice was calm and slow. *"Do not take your eyes off of the fish. Balance and breathe. Let everything disappear except you and your target. Focus . . ."*

Whitmore inhaled through his nose, his eyes fixed on the wound in the creature's back. It was smaller than the carp he and his father used to fish for on the river, but it was big enough.

He had lived two lives. As fresh breath entered his lungs, the former mercenary felt the death of one and the revival of another.

"Breathe. It doesn't know you're here. Twist your hips. Let your arm follow through. Let your body do the work."

The time was now.

Whitmore threw the spear. The tip plunged through the open wound, sparking pain and outrage from the beast. The fire coral fungus, mushed into a wet, watery substance, spat its poison into the bug's bloodstream. It spun on its legs for several moments, unable to reach the spear with its pincers. Its tail ultimately did the job, smacking the object from its body.

Slowing down, it faced the tree where the spear had come from.

Whitmore gulped. There was no way of knowing if the toxin was enough to kill the thing. Except for its death.

It was very much alive, and eager to get payback on the crafty human. Whitmore crouched and clung to one of the branches as the bug charged. Clumsy and lacking depth perception, it ran straight into the tree, stalling itself for one critical moment before scaling its height.

Whitmore leapt over it, landing on the ground with a somersault. He turned around and sprayed the contents of his AK-74 at the creature. Alarmed, it sprang off the tree and darted into the jungle, circling back after retreating several yards.

With the gun empty, Whitmore had nowhere to go but out to sea. He turned on his heels and sprinted for the ocean, crossing the beach in under three seconds.

Two seconds later, he was waist-deep in water.

The bug emerged from the jungle and stopped after realizing its prey was swimming out to sea. Whitmore was neck-deep when he finally looked back and saw the bewildered thing on the sand. For an instant, it seemed not to know what to do. There was a temptation to hurl insults at the thing—a temptation which ended immediately. The bug braved the waters. To Whitmore's shock and amazement, it moved at a remarkable speed.

He backstroked, only delaying the inevitable. The bug moved like an eel, its tail moving back and forth. The pincers yawned open, their arms rearing back to grab him.

It stopped. A bubbly substance oozed from its jaws. The legs, which paddled its body like oars, slowed drastically. Saliva and more of this foamy substance spat from its mouth.

Whitmore continued backstroking, watching the struggle the thing was enduring.

Snarling, it pushed through this discomfort and came at him again. Now, there was yellow blood coming out of its mouth. Despite this, it still advanced, claws open.

Whitmore clenched his teeth, bracing for the pain of razor-sharp claws dicing him up.

No such pain occurred. The paddling ceased, the claws locked in place in front of the creature's head. Driven by momentum, its body drifted. Whitmore paddled out of its way, watching as the enormous black body sailed past him.

It was stiff and motionless, the toxins having taken their toll. Slowly, it sank to the bottom.

It was extinct again.

"Well done."

Whitmore took in another breath and smiled. It was done not only in victory, but in cherishment of a valued memory.

"Thanks, Dad."

From here, he swam to the cove where his supplies were stored. As he went, he noticed Chinese helicopters departing from the northern part of the island. He knew the formation. They were clearing out, the operation scrapped. Soon, the island would be bombed to hell, ensuring the destruction of any remaining offspring and hosts.

As Whitmore neared the landing site, he pulled the flash drive from his pocket. No way was that thing going to come back into existence, not if he had anything to say about it.

He dropped it and let it sink to the seabed. As far as the C.I.A. was concerned, it had been lost with Lee, burned by the explosions. He would endure days' worth of debriefing at minimum, in which he would deny any knowledge of the U.S. government's involvement with the project. With a little luck, they would have to set him free.

For once, he was confident that luck was on his side.

He swam to shore, collected his gear, then set out on the long journey to the extraction site.

22

The place had never changed.

The back and side yards were comprised of three acres of bright green grass-covered land. The house was two stories, the front living room window six feet across, giving view to the sofa and fireplace inside.

There was a Ford F-350 in the driveway, its bed filled with supplies for work. A couple hundred feet behind the house was the shed. Its doors were open, the center space empty where the lawnmower usually sat. Even from this distance, Whitmore could see the rack where his old man kept his fishing rods. Next to them were two throwing spears. The sight brought a smile to his face.

He could hear the mower coming around the back corner of the house. At its wheel was Dad. At seventy-three, the man could have easily passed for someone in his late fifties. He looked toward the visitor in the driveway, smiling with pleasant surprise.

Mr. Karn switched off the mower and approached his son.

"Hi, James."

Whitmore smiled again. It was the first time in years he had heard his real name.

"Hi, Dad." He gave the place another affectionate look. "Thought I'd stop by."

His dad put a hand on his shoulder. "Well, you know you're always welcome home."

They shared a hug and went to the house.

Printed in Great Britain
by Amazon

27272493R00089

Printed in Great Britain
by Amazon